NATALIE MICHAELS
THE LAST GIRL

vinci
BOOKS

By Natalie Michaels

Steve Campbell Psychological Suspense Thrillers

The Last Girl
The Bone Forest
The White Dahlia

Vinci Books

vinci-books.com

Published by Vinci Books Ltd in 2025

1

Copyright © Natalie Michaels 2024

The author has asserted their moral right to be identified as the author of this work in accordance with the Copyright, Designs and Patents Act 1988.
This work is a work of fiction. Names, characters, places and incidents are the product of the author's imagination or are used fictitiously. Any resemblance to actual persons, living or dead, places and incidents is entirely coincidental.
All rights reserved. No part of this publication may be copied, reproduced, distributed, stored in any retrieval system, or transmitted in any form or by any means, including photocopying, recording, or other electronic or mechanical methods, nor used as a source for any form of machine learning including AI datasets, without the prior written permission of the publisher.
The publisher and the author have made every effort to obtain permissions for any third party material used in this book and to comply with copyright law. Any queries in this respect should be brought to the attention of the publisher and any omissions will be corrected in future editions.
A CIP catalogue record for this book is available from the British Library.
Paperback ISBN: 9781036705183

MIX
Paper | Supporting responsible forestry
FSC
www.fsc.org FSC® C018072

Printed and bound in Great Britain by Clays Ltd, Elcograf S.p.A.

Chapter One

THE CABIN

Jacob
1987

The quiet evening pierced my ears. Carefully, I climbed out of the water and onto the wooden deck without making a sound. I exhaled silently as I monitored the couple fast asleep in the boat. Tiptoeing on the wooden deck, I was careful not to stand on a creaking plank and when I reached the door, Katie stirred in the boat, mumbling someone's name. I opened the door, testing to ensure it didn't moan the wider I opened it, and slipped out.

I traversed the dark path to the house and entered. Leaving the lights off, I navigated my way around the living room, kitchen, until finally upstairs. I entered the main bedroom and found his suitcase again. Flipping through his wallet, I found what I was looking for and headed back down to the kitchen. Their food remained on the counter, waiting for them to enjoy, and I opened the pantry door.

Once done, I slipped out the front door and found a place hidden in shadows where I could see most of the house and waited. I heard cars driving on the ID-75 entering and exiting Ketchum and was grateful they were a distance away and wouldn't see me or my vehicle from the road.

It was ten at night by the time Katie and her friend staggered up the path, switching on lights as they entered the house and headed for the kitchen. Katie warmed their dinner while her friend sat at the table, waiting for her to serve him.

The itch at the back of my neck started up again, but I didn't scratch. I just rubbed the offending area and waited.

Katie dished food onto their plates and sat beside him. My body heated as I watched him eat. All was fine for a few seconds and then... he grabbed his throat. His eyes widened in horror. Red blotches formed on his face and neck. His face started swelling, along with one side of his neck. He pushed away from the table, stood up, then doubled over as if trying to expel whatever was lodged in his throat.

Katie was there to slap him on his back, but nothing helped.

Nothing would help him.

The man pointed to the stairs and then to his neck. Katie nodded and frantically ran upstairs.

Moments later, she returned, shaking her head. "There's nothing there," she cried.

Shock flashed in his eyes. He collapsed onto his knees, then fell on his chest and face, unmoving.

Katie dashed around, looking for something, but there was nothing that could help him. She fell to her knees and moved him onto his back so she could proceed with CPR, but his throat had already closed, shutting off all his air supply.

From where I stood, his face and neck had swollen to the point where his cheeks were red, round and puffy, and his eyes had bulged. While his fat lips had started turning purple.

After about ten minutes, Katie sat back on her haunches, crying into her hands.

I dropped the epinephrine injection on the ground and crushed it with my boot heel. Pushing through the branches, I approached the cabin with purpose and entered through the front door.

Katie flinched when she saw me and stood up. "Jacob, what are you doing here?" she asked, glancing nervously at me and then at her friend on the floor.

"I thought you might need some help," I said mysteriously and crossed the threshold. My clothing was still damp, and I left wet marks everywhere I stepped.

Katie backed up, glancing at me and the body. "We need to call for help," she stammered, "could you—"

"No," I yelled, shutting her up. "No more, Katie," I snapped. "You've been playing me for years. No more." I pulled the box out of my pocket and placed it gently on the counter. "I've had this for a while, waiting for the right moment to give it to you. To ask for your hand in marriage. Ever since that day in the barn, I've loved you more than anything else. I would've given you the world, anything, and everything you ever wanted. But," I paused for effect and stared into her sad, blue eyes, "you've made it perfectly clear where I stand with you."

Chapter Two

THE SECOND WEEK IN DECEMBER

Michelle
2001

Jessica combed her long blond hair and tied it in a low ponytail. She fixed her black top; the one I had bought her for her birthday with the famous Rolling Stones tongue. Then she fastened her belt and pulled on her coat. Grabbing her makeup bag, she applied eyeshadow, mascara that made her green eyes brighter, and lipstick sparingly, transforming her youthful face into a more mature look.

We had become best friends since first grade in the Ernest Hemingway School in Ketchum. Since then, we did nothing without the other. Once a month, we visited Mike, our good friend, and went to O'Brian's Pub for a few beers and a couple of games.

"How do I look?" she asked, twirling.

"Like you're twenty-two," I said, grinning. I pulled on my coat and huddled into it. "How about me?"

"Perfect," she said.

I wiped some makeup out of the corner of my eye and smiled. My eyes had thick eyeliner, highlighting my big brown eyes, and I tied my black hair in a low ponytail. I had a fair complexion and with my hair being naturally black; I looked like a porcelain doll. But I was not as beautiful as Jessica.

"Are you two wenches finished?" Mike yelled outside the bathroom. "I'm hungry, and there's a game with my name on."

"Yeah, yeah, we're done," I said, opening the door.

Mike stood in the doorjamb, blocking my way. He wore his signature black outfit; black army boots, black cargo pants, and a long sleeve black vest with a black jacket over. With his brown hair shaved close to his head, he reminded me of someone who should be in the army and not out drinking.

I waved the air in front of my nose. "You smell like weed again."

"I know. You want some?"

"No, thanks."

"Come," Jessica said, pushing past Mike, "there are men who need to buy us drinks."

"You're such a skank," Mike said, chuckling, his smile reaching his light brown eyes. If it wasn't for the gothic clothing he wore, I thought he was handsome.

"You're just jealous you can't get free drinks." She cooed.

"Whatever, now come," Mike said, jogging down the stairs. "Bye mom," he yelled into the lounge. His mom waved and continued watching her fantasy series.

We climbed into Mike's blue van, his Passion Wagon, and drove the short distance to O'Brian's Pub. It was a quaint little drinking hole where a lot of the residents frequented. The place smelled like stale ale. The bar counter was sticky from years of spillage, and the beer flowed all night long.

Mike parked the van in the only available parking spot, which was right at the back underneath the one lamppost that didn't work. We traversed the recently cleared path as snow continued falling around us.

I entered the pub first, and the heat smacked me in the face. Shivering from the sudden change in temperature, I headed for the bar and stood between two men talking about their workday.

"Oh, I'm sorry. Am I bothering you?" I asked, fluttering my eyelashes.

"No, sweetheart," the man on my right said. "But I would love to buy you a drink?"

"A beer will do," I said, smiling sweetly.

"Hey Nancy," said the same man, "get my lady friend here a beer."

"Make that two, please, kind sir," Jessica said behind me.

"Make it two," he said with a wicked grin. "And who might you be?"

"Jessica," she said, holding out her hand for him to shake.

Nancy gave us our beers.

The man stood to retrieve his wallet from his back pocket, paid, and sat down again. Jessica and I stood on either side of him and kissed him on the cheek.

"Thank you," we said together and disappeared into the crowd near the back, where Mike was already playing a game of pool.

We laughed and joked around. We tampered with

Mike's cue stick every time he tried to take a shot, sipped from his friends' drinks, and enjoyed our evening.

I loved coming here, as did Jessica. We were together, we always had fun, and we never had to pay for anything.

"I feel like a shot," Jessica said, swaying slightly.

"You've had enough," I said, slipping my arm through hers. "How about we ask Nancy for something to eat and two glasses of water?"

"Nah, I want a shot." Jessica unhooked her arm from mine and made a beeline toward the bar. She bumped into a man wearing a blue jacket sitting at the bar and started talking to him. She laughed at whatever he said and sat beside him. They seemed to enjoy each other's company and now and then, Jessica would touch his arm or laugh at whatever he said. Then she thumbed over her shoulder at me. But the man didn't turn around.

Mike cut in front of me, blocking my view. "Move," I moaned and pushed past him. When I could see Jessica again, she downed a shot with the man and then he stood up from his stool. He pointed at the door, and Jessica nodded.

"What are you doing?" I mumbled to myself.

"Where are you going?" Mike asked.

"To stop Jessica from making a big mistake."

"She's a big girl. She can take care of herself."

"She's only nineteen, Mike," I grumbled. "We need to look out for each other."

Mike raised his hands in mock surrender. "Fine, but if you aren't here when I'm ready to go, I'll leave your ass here, too."

I rolled my eyes and headed for the door. Jessica and the man had already left by the time I pulled on my coat. I opened the door, and the cold air stole my breath as I braved the chilly night.

A car's engine rumbled to life in the distance, and I turned to look, but couldn't see much. A light came on and I squinted.

"Jessica?" I yelled and headed for the car. "Jessica?" I yelled again, waving my arms so she could see me.

A car door slammed, and a figure headed my way. "Michelle," Jessica said, closing the gap. "I'm going home with my new friend." She wiggled her eyebrows. "I'll see you at Mike's tomorrow," she slurred, hugging me. When she let me go, her now dull green eyes glazed over as she smiled.

"Are you sure you're in condition to go home with anyone?" I asked.

"Relax, I'm fine. Besides, everyone knows him," she said, turning around.

"Who is he?" I asked. There were moments like now when I hated going out with Jessica. She had gone home with guys once or twice before, but I had always met them beforehand. I didn't know who this guy was, and it left me worried.

"It's fine, he's fine, I'm fine," she mumbled. "I'll see you in the morning." She waved over her shoulder as she walked to his car.

"Who is he?" I yelled, but she didn't hear me.

Once Jessica climbed into his car, he turned around, blinding me with his headlights. Once I could see again, all I saw were his taillights in the distance.

I didn't like her going off with some stranger she had only just met and even though he was someone everybody knew, apparently; I didn't know who he was.

Something didn't sit right with me, but I shook off the bad feeling. She was a young adult and could handle herself.

When I went back inside the pub, I had sobered up and asked Mike if we could leave. He handed me the keys and asked me to drive.

Once back at his place, I settled into the bed beside him, and he started snoring; I laid awake with worry.

The next morning, when Jessica didn't come home, I asked Mike to take me to the police station. I waited to speak with an officer, filled out forms, and explained what had happened.

When Monday came and went and Jessica still hadn't come home, and I hadn't heard from the detective, I went back to the police station. They reassured me they were investigating and would give me feedback by Wednesday.

Wednesday passed, and the detective called me on Thursday to let me know they had no leads or witnesses. He also informed me that there were many people at O'Brian's Pub and Nancy didn't remember Jessica or me being there, therefore nobody knew who the man was she had gone home with.

When Friday arrived and I still had heard nothing, I asked Mike to go with me to the pub, but because Christmas was next Tuesday, he was taking his mother to visit his aunt in Sun Valley.

I went alone to the pub, but it was empty, with only a few patrons; none of them remembered me and I couldn't recall them either. I came home early and vowed to go the next weekend and the next until I found out who Jessica's kidnapper was.

The Last Girl

If he was local, he had to return.

Chapter Three

TOUGHEN UP

Jacob - 8 years old
1974

Mama had a headache and didn't join us at church today. Papa told me we had to hurry home because he needed to tend to the sheep.

"I need to use the bathroom," I said, shifting uncomfortably in the backseat.

"We'll be home soon," Papa said, slowing the car as we drove through the town. He waved at Kip and Gladys, who worked at the Ketchum post office. I found it strange they were at work since they rarely opened on a Sunday.

I ground my teeth when Papa went over a bump, rocking the car. "Papa, please, can you stop? I need to use the bathroom."

"Toughen up, boy, we're almost home."

Tears welled in my eyes. Pain erupted in my tummy.

"Oh Jesus, fine, I'll stop at the gas station."

As Papa stopped the car, I bolted out, but I didn't make it to the bathroom in time. I stopped a stone's throw away from the door that led to the men's bathroom. The warm urine ran down my leg, in my shoe, and absorbed into the dry sand.

"Oh shucks," Papa said beside me, "it looks like you didn't make it after all. You can be lucky you didn't do that in my car." He chuckled. "I would've beaten you so badly if you messed in my car."

"Jacob wet his pants. Jacob wet his pants," three boys sang as they passed us on their bicycles. They were from my class and I knew they would tease me at school tomorrow again.

My cheeks heated, and I covered my crotch area with my hands. I glanced up at Papa, who still grinned down at me.

"Come, you've already wet yourself. Might as well climb into the car like that." Papa climbed into his car and started the engine. He glanced over his shoulder, staring at me.

Heat rose into my chest, and neck and I fisted my little hands.

"Move it," he yelled.

I stomped toward the car, opened the door, and climbed inside, slamming the door closed. My cold, damp pants stuck to my skin, making me shiver. I folded my arms across my chest, and I didn't want to look at him.

"You will become a man one day and you need to stand up for yourself," Papa said, glancing at me in his rear-view mirror now and then while he drove. "And one of those things is managing your bladder. You can't go around pissing your pants."

"Yes, Papa," I said, glancing out of the window. Our farm was on the outskirts of Ketchum, a quiet mountain town far from any city, yet close enough that one didn't want to go anywhere. Mountains surrounded our town with crystal clear waterways, hiking, and biking trails, and when it snowed everybody went skiing.

"And you need to stand up to those boys," Papa said. "They're going to bully you."

I didn't want to talk to him anymore, so I continued glancing out of the window, watching the world go by.

We passed the local cemetery where they had buried Ernest Hemingway. Mama had told me a story about the famous author and how he killed himself. They diagnosed him with some disease I couldn't pronounce. His father, sister and brother also killed themselves; I hoped I didn't get what they had.

Papa turned onto the dirt road leading up to our farmhouse and relief washed over me; I could take a nice bath and put on dry clothing. I wrinkled my nose at the smell of my urine-stained pants.

When Papa stopped the car, I climbed out and sprinted up the path toward the house, then stopped when Papa called me.

"Hurry, boy, you have chores to do."

"Yes, Papa," I said, climbing up the veranda stairs. When Papa was no longer looking at me, I bolted through the open front door, slamming it behind me. Then ran up the stairs to my bedroom and peeled the wet clothing from my body, throwing them in the laundry basket.

Hushed voices sounded outside my bedroom door, and then water started running in the bath.

There was a soft knock on my door. "Jacob," Mama said, slowly opening the door. "I've run your bath water."

"Thank you," I said, pulling off my damp underwear. "Sorry," I said, averting my eyes.

"It's ok, my son. Perhaps you should've gone before you left church."

"I wanted to, but Papa said to hurry."

She stared down at me with an expression I didn't understand. "Try harder next time because it will be difficult to clean your shoes." She picked up my soiled clothing and shoes and exited. "Hurry and bathe, your father needs you outside."

"Mama?"

She stopped and glanced over her shoulder. "What is it?"

"Why is Papa so hard on me?" I asked, my bottom lip trembling slightly.

Mama opened her mouth to say something but closed her mouth instead.

"Moira!" Papa yelled from downstairs. "Where's my boots?"

"In the closet near the front door."

"Now why did you move it there."

Mama rolled her eyes. "You left them there, Bill," she yelled.

"Don't talk back to me like that, woman."

"Yes, dear," she said, then turned back to me. "Honey," she started, then stopped as if there was something she wanted to say. "Never mind. Now hurry and be a good boy and go do your chores like Papa wants."

"Ok," I said and ran into the bathroom, slamming the door shut. I washed as quickly as possible, dried, and put on my work clothing. I didn't want Papa yelling at me again today.

The chore Papa had left for me to do was what I hated doing the most; to clean the chicken coop. But once that was done, I sat under my favorite oak tree that stood on a small hill a distance away from the farmhouse.

Papa's sheep roamed freely, grazing everything they could find.

I sat by the tree and watched the sunset. It was the first time this afternoon that I felt better after messing my pants. I felt safer and calmer out here.

Something moved out of the corner of my eye and I glanced in that direction. A wild hare sat staring at me. Slowly, I stood up and approached. The hare waited. I pounced. I caught the hare by its tail with my left hand and dug my fingernails into its body with my right hand.

I gritted my teeth as I applied more pressure. The hare made strange growling hissing sounds as it tried to get away. And I squeezed harder until bones broke.

Once I had secured the hare in my hands, I stood up. With one hand gripping it, I pulled the string out of my pocket and wrapped it around its neck. I tied the knot, ensuring the string was tight, and tied the other end of the string around a tree branch.

I watched the hare suffer while it died. There was something primitive yet satisfying about what I had done. I didn't understand it, only that I enjoyed it and wanted to do it again.

Chapter Four

JUST ANOTHER SATURDAY (EARLY JANUARY)

Jack
2002

Once a week I drove my classic Corvette into Ketchum.

Once a week I bought groceries.

Once a week I showed my face to everyone I knew so that they didn't forget who I was and what me and my family meant to this town.

But first I trimmed my hair. I used one of those luxury men's electric clippers for the back and then trimmed the top using a pair of scissors to keep everything neat. I didn't like it when hair grew over my ears; it always reminded me of Papa who used to shave my head once a week. He had said it was to ensure I had no lice because I attended school. And now, I hated having my hair so short; but I always kept it neat.

While I showered, I alternated the temperature from hot to cold while I jerked myself off; there was nothing better than fantasizing about my *Keys*; the different temperatures sent a shock throughout my body. I never came, though; which only made the experience that much more sensual later on.

I dressed in jeans, a collar shirt, white socks, and clean sneakers. I fastened my leather belt, and made sure I was presentable when I glanced at myself in the mirror before heading to the kitchen.

I made breakfast; two scrambled eggs and one slice of toast with slices of tomato on the side, and a glass of milk. My knife and fork were neatly in place, with the plate perfectly in the middle. I glanced up at the head of the table and waited, nodded, picked up my utensils, and started eating.

When my plate and glass were empty, I washed them quickly and placed them on the drying rack. I straightened the cloth on the sink I used to wipe the counter and table clean, and washed my hands. While I dried them, I glanced at the clock; it was 9 a.m..

I opened the basement door and called down to my lovely *Keys*. "I'm just going into town. Remember the rules, ladies, and I'll see you before lunchtime." I closed the basement door, locking it.

Rubbing the keys between my fingers, I couldn't wait to get back to spend some time with my *Keys*. I grabbed the Corvette's keys and traversed the path toward the area where I parked the cars; the Corvette I'd had for many years, and the dark gray Ford Explorer I'd purchased last year.

Everybody in town loved the Corvette; it was black, sleek, and a magical ride.

My first stop was the post office, where I greeted Kip and Gladys. They had worked here for as long as I could remember. I asked about their grandkids and how work was.

"Oh, you know," Gladys said, handing me the stamps I would never use. I had an entire stack of them in a drawer at home. "The kids are getting older and I'm getting grayer." She laughed.

Kip leaned on the counter. "That girl was in here again."

"What girl?" I asked.

"That Michelle girl," Kip said. "Her friend went missing before Christmas and she was in here putting up another poster." He jerked his chin toward the board. I glanced over my shoulder at the lovely Jessica, and it warmed my chest to see her smiling. I remembered that wonderful evening with her. I licked my lips.

"Poor girl gone missing," I said, taking my change. I still paid with cash, I had no cards.

"Yep," Gladys said sadly.

"Anyway, thanks for these," I said, raising the stamps. "You kind folks have a wonderful day."

"You too," they said at the same time.

"See you next week," I said, heading outside. I passed the trashcan, glanced around, and threw the stamps away. I didn't feel like holding onto them today and climbed into my car.

I drove around the corner and stopped at the grocery store where I bought my weekly supplies for home. The store was owned by Stuart Dawes, who inherited it from his father.

I entered the store, rubbing my fingers against the *Keys* and smiled. "Hi Stuart," I said, grabbing a basket. "How's business?"

"Hey Jack," Stuart said, standing up from his chair and

placing his newspaper down. "Good, how are the sunflowers?"

"Blooming," I said, grabbing a loaf of bread. "And thanks again for that contact. My glass greenhouse works perfectly." It cost me a small fortune building the greenhouse, but it was worth the money.

"Great," Stuart said, nodding and smiling. "Glad I could help you for a change."

"They're blooming beautifully while the snow falls," I said, remembering when my flowers bloomed a couple of days ago when it was so cold.

I entered the next aisle for canned food, eggs, and from the fridge three cartons of milk, fresh foods, and meat. My *Keys* already had their food, which I ordered online and had delivered directly to the farm. I didn't want anyone seeing the amount of food I ordered if it was only me at home.

I paid for the food. "See you next week," I said, grabbing the bags.

"Bye," Stuart said, picking up his newspaper.

I walked past the barbershop but never entered. Nobody but me touched my hair.

I waved at a few people I'd most likely see at O'Brian's Pub tonight while rubbing my *Keys* in my pocket and climbed into the corvette. I placed the groceries on the seat beside me and started the engine.

Once home, I unpacked the groceries and headed down to my basement. I'd decided that today it would be *Key* number 7, Maggie Tipping. I hadn't been with her in a while.

Yes, she would be my choice for today.

"Hi Maggie," I said, entering her room.

The lovely Maggie sat up like a good girl and smiled lovingly at me.

"Did you wash up, eat your food, and do your daily exercises?"

She nodded excitedly.

"Good, now assume the position," I said, reaching for her.

Maggie changed her position from sitting to kneeling and waited for me.

I locked the door behind me and closed the gap. I unzipped my pants and reached for her head, gripping her ponytail tightly in my right hand, and pulled her closer, her mouth opening for me.

I came for Maggie. It was the ultimate gift for her. I only came for my *Keys*; it was my tribute to them; for them; because of them. Everything I did was for my *Keys*.

I wiped myself on a towel I had brought with, kissed Maggie on her forehead and smiled when she laid back down.

I locked the door behind me, touching her room number, and thanked her.

I ascended the stairs two at a time and entered the bathroom to wash up, then got ready for my evening at O'Brian's Pub.

Chapter Five

EARLY JANUARY

Michelle
2002

It's been three weeks since Jessica disappeared and it's driving me crazy. The police have no leads. Nancy from O'Brian's Pub in Ketchum couldn't recall who Jessica had left with, and the owner, Pat, didn't have any cameras outside of his pub.

"I'm sorry I couldn't be of more help," Detective Campbell said on the other side of the line.

"Thanks, Detective. Is there anything else I can do?" I asked, feeling hopeful.

"No, and I'll let you know the moment we learn something new."

"Ok, bye," I said, feeling sad again, and hung up before Detective Campbell did.

"What did he say?" Mike asked, eating a bread stick.

"No one has seen her. Nobody knows who this man is," I said, grabbing a bread stick he offered. "There were too many people that night because nobody remembers anything. Everything is a dead end."

"What now?" he asked.

"I don't know."

We were silent for a moment.

"You went to the pub before Christmas and it was empty, but things are back to normal now. How about we go to the pub every night until we see something?"

"I don't know what he looks like," I said, my brows scrunching together.

"True," he said, his mouth full of food. "But he doesn't know that."

I fell silent as I considered his words. I could go to O'Brian's and wait for this creep to approach me first, since I didn't know what he looked like. Perhaps he would remember me when I asked everyone there that I was searching for Jessica. Yeah. This might work.

Chapter Six

KATIE

Jacob - 11 years old
1977

I watched Katie approach. She stopped to speak with Mr. Williams, our Head Master of Ketchum Elementary, then headed for her locker.

"Hey, idiot," said a boy behind me.

I flinched and spun around in time to block his elbow from hitting my jaw.

"What are you staring at, hmm?" Dylan sneered, glancing her way. "Oh, so the idiot of the school likes the new girl. Pity she'll never get to know you." With his parting words, he pushed my head against the lockers behind me and punched me in the chest.

I winced, rubbing my chest.

The bell sounded, and everyone headed for the cafeteria. I sighed and pulled my brown lunch bag out of my locker, closed the door, and ensured I locked it. Last week,

Dylan found it open and threw all my belongings in the trash.

I headed for my usual table right at the back of the cafeteria and sat down. Mama had made another peanut butter and jelly sandwich. I groaned after having a bite; it was the third time this week. I was about to roll my eyes when Katie headed my way.

My little heart thundered inside my eleven-year-old chest. There were no exits near my table, yet she was coming my way. She stared at me the entire time and I fought not to look behind me for fear she would disappear. My damp palms itched, and I wiped them on my pants.

"Can I sit here?" Katie said, her smile reaching her eyes.

I stood up and pulled out a chair. "Yes, yes, please sit," I said, mumbling my words. I waited for her to sit, like Papa did for Mama, and then I sat. My eyes trained on her. I swallowed hard and my throat was dry. I picked up my soda, my hand shaking, and enjoyed a warm sip; anything was better than nothing, even if it was warm.

"My name is Katie," she said, still smiling.

"Jacob," I said, holding out my hand for her to shake. Papa had said I should always shake hands with someone new, even if it was a girl; it was a sign of respect. We shook once and as much as I wanted to keep holding her soft, warm hand, I let go. "Why are you sitting here?" I asked, glancing around, but nobody paid us any attention.

"Why not?" she asked with a shrug. "I don't bite."

I snorted, cupping the soda that squirted out of my nose in my hand. I picked up a napkin and wiped my face and hand. "It's not that, it's just…" I left my words hanging. How could I tell the new girl she was sitting with the person nobody wanted to be friends with?

"I like you, Jacob," she said. "You have kind blue eyes,

and I've seen how they bully you, and that's just wrong. They're mean." She picked up her sandwich and had a bite, leaving mayo on the corners of her mouth, which she licked away. "So, if you don't mind us being friends?" Her eyes twinkled with humor.

I nodded and bit into my peanut butter and jelly sandwich. "I'd like that."

We ate our sandwiches in a comfortable silence I had never experienced before and I liked it. We stole glances at each other and smiled awkwardly. It was fun.

I rubbed my growing erection; the sensation sending warmth throughout my body, and I shuddered. I couldn't help my growing smile as wonderful thoughts came to me; perhaps Katie could be my wife one day.

"Did you enjoy your first week?" I asked Katie as we walked home together.

"It's been good," she said, smiling, but it didn't reach her eyes. She fell silent for a moment, then turned to look at me. "You've been in Ketchum your whole life?"

I nodded. "Yep, and my parents, grandparents, and great grandparents. Why?"

"My dad promised us that when we moved, he would be home more, but that hasn't happened. He's working more now than he ever did."

"What does your mom say?"

"She isn't happy. She fights with my dad often and started smoking again. And drinking." She kicked pebbles, and they skittered across the sidewalk. She glanced up when we reached her house and we watched Sheriff Adams exit their house, fixing his hat.

"What is he doing here?" I asked, frowning.

"No idea," she said, opening the small gate and traversed up the path to the front door.

The sheriff drove off, not seeing us.

Katie inserted her key, and the door clicked open. She opened the door halfway, then stopped, turning toward me. "Would you like to come in?"

"Nah, I need to go work on the farm. My father doesn't like it when I'm home late from school," I said, fixing my backpack.

Screams sounded behind me, and I glanced over my shoulder. Dylan and his friends cycled past, whistling at a mother and daughter walking across the road. A chilly feeling washed over me at the thought of bumping into him again. Since becoming friends with Katie, he had left me alone.

"See you tomorrow morning, then?" she said, looking at the boys cycling. "If he comes after you, go into a yard and scream for help."

I turned back to look at her, but she was scowling at Dylan, and I couldn't help but smile. "Good advice," I said, turning around and heading for the sidewalk. "I'll see you tomorrow." I waved over my shoulder.

Our farm was on the outskirts of Ketchum, with only a dirt road going in and out. I'd walked this road every day by myself since first grade. I knew where the ditches were by heart, along with the location of most of the wild rabbit burrows. There were wildflowers growing on the left-hand side of the dirt road, while on the right many poisonous flowers blossomed. I knew everything about this road.

The Last Girl

Our double story house, which one could see from the road, reminded me of the plantation houses from Louisiana. My great-grandparents had built the large house hoping to fill it with many grandchildren, but they only had one son, who had one son, who had me.

The house had lavish furnishings for the times and I loved living here, but it was the two stories below ground that frightened me. The basement held the washing area and the boiler, and the next level below that had little rooms where I used to play and hide. It had small open rooms with dirt flooring. The rooms reminded me of a stable but underground, and I often wondered whether my great grandfather wanted to build another area where he could do his woodworking. But it was terribly dark down there and had most likely abandoned the idea.

"Hey idiot," Dylan screamed behind me, bringing me out of my thoughts. His bicycle kicking up sand and stones along the way. "Are you going to mommy to kiss your booboo?" he taunted.

Dylan had never come this way before, which meant he was here on purpose. It had been a week since he had last bothered me and after years of his torment, I'd had enough. Today would be the day I would stand my ground. If Dylan tried anything with me now, I would gladly hit him back.

"Why are you like this, Dylan?" I asked, fisting my hands. "I've done nothing to you. Are you jealous of me?"

Dylan came to a skidding stop, and I covered my face to avoid eating his dust. "As if," he harrumphed. He leaned forward and pushed me. "I just don't like you, weasel."

I didn't know what came over me, but I swung my backpack at him, knocking him off his bicycle, but he managed to stay upright. He groaned as he shielded his face with his forearms when I swung my backpack again. He fell, hitting the dirt hard with his bike on top of him. I dropped my bag and leaped onto the frame of the bike, keeping him down.

"I've had enough," I said through gritted teeth. "Leave me alone, or else..."

"Or else what?" he taunted. His smile stretched his face, reaching his dark eyes, and he licked the blood off his bottom lip. "Your mama should've put a dress on you," he sneered.

An anger I had never felt before flooded my system. Heat crept up my legs, through my abdomen and arms, up my neck and heated my cheeks. My fingernails dug into my palms, and sweat dripped down my back.

With my weight on the bicycle frame near his neck, I jumped again; the metal striking his throat. I leaned forward so that the frame pressed hard against his throat. I trapped one of his hands beneath the bicycle frame, and he tried pushing me off using his other hand, but I was stronger for once. He made a strange, strangling noise as his eyes bulged. I started bouncing on the bike and the cold metal frame kept striking his throat, crunching bones. He spat blood. His hand dropped limply to his side, and his eyes rolled into the back of his head.

I jumped one last time onto the bike to make sure he would never hurt me again and he just laid there, unmoving, and unseeing.

A strange sense of satisfaction washed over me like a bucket of warm water, making me shudder with delight. I climbed off the bicycle frame and stood beside his body, staring down at him, and smiled. It was a relief he would no longer hurt me or anybody else ever again.

Chapter Seven

POTENT PLANTS

Jacob - 11 years old
1977

Standing near Dylan's body, a pretty flower caught my attention; in the shape of a large square grew a variety of poisonous flowers. It seemed too random that they grew here and what looked like rows, as if someone had planted them here for a purpose.

Mama had shown me pictures of the flowers I had to avoid so that I didn't touch them and get sick by accident. I remembered thinking how interesting they were, that a flower so beautiful could be so deadly, and I wanted to know more about them.

I grabbed my empty lunch bags and without touching them, carefully picked the pretty purple flowers of nightshade, the deep purple of Delphinium, white Jimsonweed, pink Foxglove, white bell-shaped Lily of the valley, a variety of pink Oleander, and white poison Hemlock.

There was a black flower that grew on its own that I'd

never seen before. It had a tall stem and the flower part looked like a dress, with two flowers in the center. It was pretty, but I knew if I ingested it, it would cause me harm.

Once I had a sample of each flower, I placed them carefully in my backpack so that they didn't bend or break and headed home. I wanted to read up on them again and find out exactly the damage they caused.

Chapter Eight

THE SECOND SATURDAY IN JANUARY

Michelle
2002

My car idled, blowing warm air into my face. I shivered watching the snow fall onto my windscreen and muttered under my breath for spring to hurry.

I'd parked my car outside of O'Brian's Pub, and watched the patrons park and enter. None of the men seemed familiar, and I started questioning my memory and what I saw the evening Jessica had disappeared. I couldn't be sure he was even a man, but I knew Jessica. I knew the type of person she preferred; it was a man, and I should stop doubting myself.

He took Jessica on the second Saturday in December last year and today was the second Saturday in January, and the police still had found nothing. There were no clues, no witnesses, no DNA for them to test. Nothing. They couldn't do anything, and it frustrated me.

That's why I was here. It was up to me to do something.

I sighed a frustrated breath, leaned into my seat, and closed my eyes for a second. It was early still. I would enter the pub round about the same time we did that awful night and hopefully the man who had taken her recognized me and approached me. I hoped.

So, resting now a bit wouldn't hurt.

The rumble of the engine cut out, and I jolted awake. I blinked at the red battery light flashing on the dash. "No!" I cried out, glancing around. The parking lot was dark, with only a few lights illuminating the area. The snow covered my windscreen and the clock on the dash read 12:08.

I couldn't believe I had fallen asleep and had slept for four hours, I chastised myself as I wiped sleep out of my eyes. "Come, start for me," I said as I turned the key, but the engine made that metallic clicking, grinding sound. The radio flared to life, only to die a dismal death once more. "Crap," I grumbled, smacking the steering wheel, and winced because I'd hurt my hand.

I turned toward the laughter, and a group of men exited the pub, hanging onto each other's shoulders as they made their way to their cars.

There were so many trucks and vehicles outside someone had to have a jump lead I could use. I buttoned my coat to the top and pulled on my gloves. I climbed out, slammed the door, and walked toward the entrance.

Blood circulated throughout my body, and I felt warmer. I opened the pub door and stale, warm air hit me in the face, along with a stink of fried onions. "Yuck," I mumbled to myself, and swallowed hard.

The pub was more crowded than I had ever seen it before. People were chatting, laughing, eating, and drinking. Some danced, while others played pool in the back.

The Last Girl

A loving couple sat at a table near the door, lost in each other's eyes, and I couldn't help myself from smiling at them. Then reality set in, and I grumbled under my breath.

I dusted snow off my shoulders, kept my coat on, and headed for the bar where Nancy served a group of females enjoying a bachelorette party.

I sat on a bar stool beside a man enjoying his burger. He glanced up at me and smiled. I smiled back. Something behind the man caught my eye and another man wearing a navy jacket that looked similar to what Jessica's kidnapper wore and I was about to follow him, but then he went to the bathroom. The last thing I wanted to do was follow any man into a stall by myself. Me being here was a risk, but I wasn't stupid and would never willingly put my life in danger... yet.

"I haven't seen you here before," the man eating the burger said.

I glanced at him again and offered a half smile. "No, only driving through, but my car died and I need someone with jump leads to help me." I stood up, ready to call Nancy for help.

He smiled kindly and his blue eyes twinkled. "I can help you, miss. Allow me to finish my dinner and I'll get you on the road in no time."

"Thank you," I said, sitting down again.

Nancy approached and smiled at me. "What can I get you?" she asked, then did a double take. "Aren't you the girl who keeps coming in here looking for her friend?"

The man beside me sat straight, staring at me.

"Yeah, but that's not why I'm here tonight."

"Don't worry, Nancy. I'll take care of the girl," the man said, wiping his mouth clean.

Chapter Nine

YOU NEVER FORGET YOUR FIRST

Jacob
1982

I'd just finished my chores when Mama called me for lunch. I placed my gloves on the table, washed my hands—twice, and sat down. My tummy grumbled when the smell of bacon and eggs wafted in the air, my mouth salivating, but I waited patiently.

Papa entered the room, kissed Mama on her cheek, then looked at me, nodding once. He sat at the head of the table with a loud sigh.

I knew that sigh. It was a sigh that said too much; it was a sigh that told me I didn't do exactly what Papa wanted me to do. That I'd messed up, according to him.

"Jacob," he said my name with anger in his voice. "You didn't do your chores as per my instruction."

"I did, Papa—"

"Don't interrupt me," he yelled, slamming his fists on

the table. Mama flinched, glancing at me and then Papa. The lines between his eyes deepened and his neck started spotting red. "You fed the cows late. You didn't sweep. And the barn is still a mess."

I fisted my hands. I did everything he had asked me to do.

"And because of this, you lose your pocket money for the week."

"I finished my chores, Papa," I whined. "I did everything you asked. And I did sweep—"

Mom set his plate of food in front of him, moving it so that it was correctly in place. She remained standing near him, waiting for his approval.

"You didn't do it properly, boy," Papa grunted. "You're sixteen and need to learn how to do your chores like a man. If you had been watching me like you're supposed to, you would know how to do things around here. But I guess I can't trust you." He picked up his fork and had a small bite. He nodded and Mama fetched our plates.

"You just don't want me to buy the stereo and records," I grumbled, folding my arms across my chest. He had been promising me for a year that he would help me buy these items, but every time I was close to having enough money, he made up an excuse not to give it to me.

"Maybe next time your attitude will improve and will do your chores properly. But until then, no, I won't be buying that for you."

I wished I could slam my fist into his face just so he could feel some pain. Just so he could feel something. I fisted my hands until they ached.

Mama moved the plate so that it was in its perfect spot in front of me and sat down with her plate perfectly where it should be. We waited. Father scooped more food into his mouth and only when he was halfway did he say we could eat, but I'd already lost my appetite. Mama kicked me softly under the table, arching an eyebrow. I groaned inwardly and picked up my fork.

We ate in silence. I was too angry to speak, and my parents were avoiding each other's gazes.

I flinched when Papa spoke. "After lunch, you are to do your chores again. Do you understand me?" he said sternly. "And I'll think about giving you pocket money."

"Yes, sir," I said, finishing my food as quickly as I could. I excused myself, picked up the plate, and placed it inside the sink, then exited through the kitchen toward the barn.

I would tend to my chores shortly, but first I wanted to see how my flowers were growing. I entered the barn and headed for my corner, where various plants grew in their pots on shelves near a window; Nightshade, Delphinium, Jimson weed, Foxglove, Lily of the valley, Oleander, and poison Hemlock.

That day Dylan had followed me home was the day I dug up some of the lethal flowers to understand them a little better. I borrowed books from the library so that I knew exactly what each potent plant did to a human body. It was all very interesting.

From each, I created a type of oil from the flower and stem, then injected it into animals to understand what quantity worked the quickest.

Nightshade, if used in moderation, had a type of muscle relaxant and anti-inflammatory effect, according to the books. If I injected more than necessary, the animal experienced convulsions and died.

When I injected Delphinium into the wild hare, it killed the animal immediately. In the books, they described humans struggling to breathe and they experienced muscular weakness and trembling. I may have used too much when I tested it on the animal.

The side effects for Jimson weed were dry mouth, blurry vision, dilated pupils, confusion, and difficulty in urinating. And in severe cases, the person had seizures and ended up in a coma. After I injected a small amount into a hare, it ran around in circles and bumped into things. But it didn't die.

Foxglove was fatal. The wild hare didn't last long; it convulsed and died.

After I injected Lily of the valley into the wild hare, it stopped moving and when I felt its body, its heart threatened to burst out of its chest. It died after about fifteen minutes.

The wild hare didn't last long after I injected it with Oleander, either. It moved around as if confused, convulsed for a bit, then it stopped moving.

Poison Hemlock took about twenty minutes before the hare died. I noted it seemed confused before collapsing. The second time I tested it, I had messed some of the oil onto the hare and it had the same reaction. That pleasantly surprised me.

All my experiments were interesting and I had learned a lot. I was still in two minds about trying it on a human.

I'd just exited the barn when I saw Katie running toward me. Her face was red and her clothing creased. She slammed into me so hard, we almost fell over.

"What's wrong?" I asked with concern.

"My father," she cried, "he died in a car accident."

"When?" I said, gripping her shoulders and standing back so that I could see her face. Her blue eyes shone like crystals from her red-rimmed eyes, and tears streamed down her face. "What happened?" I asked, my tone softer, gentler.

I let go of her shoulders and reached for her hand while

she wiped tears with her free hand. We stepped inside the barn, giving us some privacy.

"Sheriff Adams came over again, and I thought he and Mom were going out when he called me over and told us the news—" she broke down in a sob and I wrapped my arms around her, bring her closer to me so she could cry into my chest. Her hair smelled fruity and her skin soft beneath my touch. I touched strands of her hair, and she didn't push my hand away.

"It's okay, let it all out. I'm not going anywhere," I said, then waited until she settled down before letting her go. "I'm sorry for your loss," I whispered against her head.

Her shoulders dropped as she wiped her face. She glanced up at me, her eyes pleading for attention.

I cupped her face and planted a delicate kiss on her lips. It was our first kiss; it was soft and delicate and very special. We had been the best of friends since we were eleven years old, had held hands before but never shared a kiss, not until now. I let her go and smiled, hopeful she could see on my face how much I cared for her. That I would be here for her whenever she needed me.

She blinked at me and touched her bottom lip. Then, when she looked up at me again, this time with a heated gaze, I kissed her again. She didn't push me away, and I took that as a sign to kiss her harder, almost bruising her lips with mine.

Katie wrapped her arms around my neck, rocked onto her toes, and pressed her breasts against my chest and her lips harder against mine. We melded into each other. I felt her heart pound against me as our hands explored each other's bodies.

I had been waiting for this moment since the first time

we met. The first time she glanced my way and sat at my table in the cafeteria, I knew she would be mine.

We continued kissing as we walked as one farther inside the barn. I didn't want Mama or Papa seeing us. She almost tripped and fell, but I was there to catch her.

I grabbed her hand and led her to a spot I used when I wanted to get away from my father and have a nap; in the corner where I kept a blanket on hay.

"This is cozy," she said breathlessly. Before I could answer, she started undressing.

My gaze raked up her naked body, and I fought hard not to tear my clothing trying to get it off.

I stripped as Katie sat on the blanket and opened her legs.

"Jacob!" Papa yelled from outside the barn.

Katie and I scrambled to get dressed in time to watch Papa storm inside the barn.

"What have you done, boy?" Papa said, anger flashing in his eyes. "Her father just died and you're out here…" He left his words hanging as he raised his hands for effect. "I hope to God you didn't rape her—"

"No Papa, it's not like that."

"You'll get a beating nonetheless," he said. His tone was a warning.

"No, sir," Katie said, buttoning her top. "He didn't hurt me."

"Good," Papa said. "And I hope there won't be a bastard child."

"No, sir," we said together.

"Katie," Papa said, "your mother wants you home."

"Yes, sir," she said, averting her eyes and stepped into her shoes. She picked up her house keys and pocketed them.

"Sorry for your loss," he said. "Your mom told us what happened. It's tragic what some selfish people do. This is why the missus and I don't drink." He shook his head and his features softened, but when he glanced my way, they hardened again. Sometimes he didn't have to tell me how disappointed he was in me. His words and glance were enough. "And it's why Jacob should never drink. He's terribly irresponsible and would kill someone, too, if he drank."

I fisted my hands and scowled at him.

Katie glanced nervously at me, then at my father. "I should go," she said softly to me, then to my dad she added, "Have a good day, Uncle Bill."

I started walking out with her and had to pass *Bill*, my *father*. I walked around him, but he purposefully stepped in my way so that our shoulders bumped.

"Don't go too far, Jacob," he warned. "There are things you need to do."

I glowered at him and grunted my response, fixing my shirt.

I reached for Katie's hand, but instead of allowing me to hold her, she flinched and stepped farther away from me. Glancing over my shoulder, I saw father staring at me with a sly smile. As if he took joy in the fact that Katie didn't want to hold my hand. That she was too embarrassed, or she didn't like me enough to hold my hand, or she didn't like me as much as I liked her.

"I'll see you tomorrow at school," Katie said as she hurried down the driveway.

"Bye," I said, standing next to the open barn door.

"What is wrong with you, boy?" Papa said behind me,

making me flinch. I didn't hear him approach and yet he stood so close to me I could feel his warm breath against my neck.

I spun around, coming face to face with him.

"Her father just died, and you do that to her," he said, thumbing behind him. "You are not good enough for her, boy. Do you understand me? You're worthless. You're a nothing," he spat.

My shoulders slumped, and I averted my eyes as my cheeks heated.

"Look at me when I speak to you, boy," Papa said through gritted teeth.

I stared at the ants crawling around on the grass when his hand connected with my cheek. I lost balance and crashed to the ground.

"Get up," he demanded.

I raised my head, but the sun was shining behind him, and I couldn't see his face. Slowly, I stood up on shaky legs and raised my chin, staring him in the eyes. Papa had dark, dead eyes; like he'd seen terrible things nobody should see, but he only looked at me that way.

"She's the one who wanted me," I said. "We love each other, Papa."

"Stupid boy," he mumbled as he turned around and headed back up the path toward the house. "A girl like that will never love someone like you."

"I'm not stupid," I yelled. "And she does love me." For the first time in my life, I didn't back down. My father was always cruel to me, but not today. Today I became a man in more ways than one. "You aren't even my real father, and I'm sick of you treating me like I'm nothing."

Bill spun around and stalked back toward me. "That's because you are nothing to me," he said, raising his hand to strike. Anger filled my veins, and I blocked his hand with my left arm and before he could retaliate, I punched him in the face with my right fist. The impact knocked his head backward. Blood sprayed down his chin and over my fist.

When Bill stood straight, tears gathered in his eyes as his nose continued bleeding. The shock registering in his gaze helped me stand taller, and I stared him straight in his eyes; he was no longer the tallest or strongest one between us.

"This is how you treat the man who feeds you—"

"And beats me," I grumbled. "You deserve much worse," I said. My tone was so deep it made my arms pebble. "If I were you, I'd start treating me better. Do you understand?"

Bill rubbed his jaw and wiped his nose with his sleeve. Then he lunged for me, but I was too quick and ran inside the barn. I grabbed the rake and spun around in time to swing and smacked him on his shoulder. He lost balance and fell against the table where the lantern burned brightly. We watched in slow motion as the glass fell and shattered on the floor, spilling its flaming contents everywhere, and the dry ground caught alight. The kerosene splashed across the hay, burning it violently.

We ran outside together, then Bill slammed the door in my face. I shoulder bumped the door open before it closed in on me; the heat from the fire beating against my back.

We scrambled for buckets, throwing water at the flames, but they burned rapidly and spread across the old wood quickly.

I was about to fill the bucket again when Bill grabbed my shirt and shook his head. "That's enough. The fire is too strong. Just stop. Let the old girl burn."

I wanted to run inside to gather my lethal plants, but he

was right. I would only hurt myself, and I could replace the plants.

We stood a distance away, sweat drenching our clothing, and we watched in silence as the old barn burned to the ground.

Bill glanced at me and there was something different registering in his eyes. Perhaps he realized he could no longer tease or beat me. That maybe I'd grown into the man who would one day fight back dirtier than he ever could, and if he wasn't careful, I would bury him beside Dylan's corpse, surrounded by various herbs and poisonous plants.

Chapter Ten

THE GOOD SAMARITAN

Michelle
2002

I followed the man outside, passing a couple of bikers with jackets that read *'Heavenly Angels Gang'* with a picture of a large angel across their backs. Their bald heads shone in the dim light and their cheeks were rosy from the Tequila they downed.

"My name is Jack," he said, glancing over his shoulder. He reached for the door, opened it, and stood to one side, allowing me to exit first.

"Michelle," I said, shaking the free hand he proffered. His cool blue eyes penetrated mine, and my smile reached my eyes. I stepped past him, and the smell of his ocean fresh cologne caressed my cheeks and heat stirred within me. "Have you always lived in town?"

"Born and raised, I'm afraid," he said, smiling kindly. "And you?"

"I'm not from Ketchum, but I have friends I visit often." We stepped out into the cold, and I huddled into myself. "Do you go to O'Brian's Pub every night?" I asked.

"Nope, usually just a Friday or a Saturday evening, depending on how I feel."

I couldn't recall seeing him the times I came here asking about Jessica. "Do you remember seeing this girl?" I asked, showing him a picture of her.

He shook his head. "No, when was she here?"

"We were here before Christmas."

"No, sorry, I don't really pay much attention to my surroundings. I just enjoy a quiet dinner and then go home."

"That's a late dinner," I said, grinning.

"It's the best time, if you ask me." Jack pointed toward his car. "That's me over there." He approached a dark gray Ford Explorer, opened the back, and pulled out a set of jump leads. "Where's your car?"

"I'm up there," I said, pointing to my car. I didn't realize I'd parked so far away or that my car drowned in shadows. A nervousness spread throughout, but I shook it off. I didn't want anyone seeing me anyway, because I was here searching for a kidnapper I had never seen before. I thought it would be best to remain in the shadows and to watch everyone. But the closer I got to my car, I realized it may not have been the best idea.

I glanced over my shoulder as Jack climbed into his car. He gave me the thumbs up, and I relaxed; I was being paranoid for no reason.

I climbed into my car and popped the hood while Jack parked the nose of his car close to mine. He opened the hood to his car and connected the jump leads to his car and then mine. "I'll let you know when to start your engine."

I nodded my understanding and climbed back inside. Jack started his car's engine again and yelled at me. I turned the key and my car flared to life, the engine purring like it always did.

"Thank you so much for helping me," I said, approaching Jack, who headed my way.

"My pleasure." He unclipped the jump leads and placed them back inside his car.

I left my car idling.

"You think you'll be okay on your own?"

"Yes, I should be fine."

"Good," he smiled again, and I couldn't help but notice his gaze raking over me. He was at least fifteen to twenty years older than me, but there was something about him that attracted me to him; his dark, neat hair, blue eyes, kind smile, powerful hands.

One thing I loved about a man was his hands, especially the veins running across the top of his tanned skin. And Jack had a way about him that oozed charm and character, which was very appealing to me.

"Let me be on my way," I said, yawning. It was past midnight, and I was exhausted. I wanted to get to Mike's place and sleep.

Jack waved goodbye and climbed into his Ford. He reversed, turned around, and slowly drove down the road. I put the car into gear and started down the road when it chugged, spluttered, and died again. The radio screeched and died too. I turned the key and the engine did that metal clicking sound again; the battery was completely dead.

Jack's truck's reverse lights came on and he closed the gap. He climbed out, rubbing his hands together for warmth, and traversed back to me. He knocked on the window and I slowly wound it down.

"Seems the old girl has had enough for one night, and I doubt a tow truck would come out at this hour. If you like, I can tow you back to my place and call someone in the morning to look at her. Does that sound okay to you?"

He was right. It was late; I was tired and cold, and with it snowing heavily, I would wait a while before a tow truck arrived.

We stared into each other's eyes and although he was a stranger; I didn't feel he was a threat.

"I could always phone my friend," I said, feeling guilty about going with Jack to his house. I felt bad enough staying by Mike so often he had even given me a key to the front door. He could fetch me, but then I remembered he was out with his other friends tonight and may sleep somewhere else, and his mom didn't drive. "Or I can walk to the motel that's up the road." Although a warm bed sounded wonderful, I didn't want to burden anyone. An evening in a motel with money I didn't really have to spend sounded worse. I sighed.

"Nonsense," Jack said. "I don't mind helping. My house is big enough and you can always let your friend know where you are," he said, glancing around. "It's getting cold, and I don't think either of us should be out all night." He huddled into his jacket, dusting snow off his nose.

"Okay, thank you, that sounds great," I said, "but only if it's not too much trouble."

"No trouble at all," he said, smiling and putting his hands in his pockets. "Let me hook you up." He opened the back of his truck and pulled out a metal rod and connected our cars. "Leave your car in neutral, otherwise we can't go anywhere." He grinned.

I climbed back into my car and did as he suggested, then waited for him to get back inside his car. His truck slowly went forward, pulling my car behind him. I turned the steering wheel when his car turned, and it surprised me my car didn't slide on the wet surface.

I couldn't see anything outside with the snow falling and everything was so dark. After about ten minutes, he turned up a dirt road I had never seen before. My brows furrowed reading the faded sign for Ketchum. I thought I knew all the roads around here, but somehow, I'd missed this one.

The cars moved slowly up the long driveway and once we reached the top of a small hill, I saw his large house in the distance. It surprised me I hadn't seen this house from the road either.

He stopped near the front of the house, climbed out, and unhooked my car. I grabbed my bag and reached for the glove compartment, opening it, then closed it again.

A knock at my window startled me and I flinched when I saw his face close to the window. "Come inside where it's warm." He crooked his finger, stepping away from my car door, and headed for the house. He glanced over his shoulder at me; I didn't know him well enough to discern his expression.

"On my way," I said, opening my car door and in that split second, I thought best to take it. I opened the glove compartment again and reached for my gun.

Chapter Eleven

THE DAY AFTER THE BARN FIRE

Jacob
1982

I couldn't wait to get to school the next morning. Yesterday, Katie came to me in tears and she left smiling. We had given each other our virginity, and I was more in love with her now than I'd ever been. I'd always known she was the one; the one I'd marry, the one I'd spend my life pleasing, the one who would share everything with me.

We had a special bond and were perfect for each other.

My smile split my face in two when I saw her approach. It was recess, and we always ate lunch together.

My heart thundered in my chest as I fought not to kiss her again. I would forever treasure her soft lips on mine, her warm skin against my body as I touched every part of her. I glanced around nervously as I adjusted myself in my pants; the last thing I needed now was to be called into the principal's office because I had an erection.

"Hi," Katie said.

"Hi, how are you doing?" I asked, pulling her into an embrace. She gently pushed me away when a teacher walked past and I let her go, feeling sad and a little confused.

"I'm okay, I guess," she said sadly. "Let's sit down."

We passed a poster of Dylan's face on the wall near the entrance to the cafeteria. Every year around the time of his "disappearance" the school displayed a poster of his face asking for information. His parents paid for it and sometimes attended school for a day to ask anyone if they knew where he was. Nobody knew… only me and I would say nothing.

We entered the cafeteria and headed for our table at the back.

"I heard there was a fire by your farm?" Katie said, biting into her cheese sandwich.

"Yeah," I said in between mouthfuls. I kept stealing glances at her, but she avoided eye contact.

"Are you okay? Is the barn ruined?" she asked, finishing the corner part of her sandwich, and dusting her hands.

After Bill and I watched the barn burn to the ground yesterday, we said nothing to each other for the rest of the day, not even when the sheriff questioned us, or during dinner with Mama crying.

I suspected Bill felt the weight of my cold stare. He was alive… for now, and he had to have known that if he did anything to hurt me again, that I wouldn't allow him to get away with it. Not anymore.

"Yeah," I said, my thoughts returning to the present. "We'll need to rebuild the barn, and I'm better now." My smile returned when I glanced at her, but she continued fidgeting with her lunch bag.

"Um, Jacob," she said, looking at me then. Her blue eyes sparkled brightly. "What happened yesterday can never happen again."

Blood whooshed in my ears as ice filled my veins. I swallowed hard and gripped the table to keep myself from falling over. An itch started at the back of my neck; it was something that had never happened before, and it intensified.

"I'm sorry, Jacob, but I prefer we remain friends."

I was silent as I considered her words. Friends. The love of my life only wanted to be *friends*. I didn't want to be friends with her; we were lovers now, and I wanted it to continue, then after school we could become husband and wife. I wanted us to spend the rest of our lives together with at least three children. We didn't even have to stay on the farm. I would live wherever she wanted to live.

She stared at me, then her brows scrunched together. There had to be more to her story.

"Do you regret what we did?" I finally asked, placing the rest of my sandwich down, no longer hungry.

"No," she said, shaking her head, "never. My father just died, and I was vulnerable—"

"Do you think I took advantage of you?" I asked, rubbing the back of my neck. The itch burned as if melting my skin and spine.

"No, no, that's not what I'm saying. Just that I was vulnerable yesterday, but from today onwards I need to focus on my schoolwork, my mom, and then help with my dad's funeral arrangements." She smiled, but it didn't reach her eyes. When she reached for my arm, I pulled away. She flinched as if I'd slapped her. "I still need you, Jacob," she said my name with so much emotion I couldn't reject her. "I still want us to be friends."

"It's confusing, Katie," I said, trying not to let my emotions take over. "We did something special yesterday and today it just feels like you…" I shrugged. I didn't want to say I felt used because Katie would never do that to me, but still. Things felt different now.

"It was very special, Jacob, and I'll forever remember it." She glanced at the noisy boys at the table next to us, then back at me. "We're better off being best friends."

I exhaled a shaky breath and reached for her hand, covering it with mine. It hurt to know she wanted nothing more than friendship, but I didn't want to lose her because my bruised ego had gotten in the way. She may not be ready now, but she would be after school; then we could grow closer as a couple. And right now, I'd do anything to keep her in my life. She was my only true friend.

"I'll always be there for you, Katie," I said, squeezing her hand reassuringly. There was one thing I had to know. "Do you regret it?" I asked.

"No," she said quickly, smiling kindly. "Not at all." She squeezed my hand. "Guess what?" she asked, changing the subject.

"What?"

"My dad's insurance was quick with the claim, and they'll be paying out. My mother is happy, of course." Then her features changed as she thought of something. "And that sheriff was still at our house when I got home yesterday afternoon." She rolled her eyes. "My father hasn't been gone for long and they're already showing how madly in love they are."

"Sorry you're going through so much," I said, leaning back in the chair. What I didn't tell her was if I had my way, I'd ensure her mom and the sheriff got what they deserved;

a space next to Dylan. I couldn't believe they flaunted their relationship like that.

"Anyway, my mom is fetching me after school, so I won't be able to walk home with you today." She stood up and cleared her part of the table. "I'll see you tomorrow." She didn't wait for my reply and left while I remained in my seat, watching her leave.

An overwhelming sadness consumed my thoughts. I'd gone from being in love with the woman of my dreams to being pushed to one side because maybe yesterday was a mistake.

It felt as if I'd lost my best friend even though I hadn't. Yet... something had changed because of yesterday and not in a good way.

Chapter Twelve

A SLICE OF PECAN PIE

Michelle
2002

Jack left his front door open, and I closed it behind me. The mirror on the wall to my right had a carved wooden frame stained a dark mahogany. It looked like an antique. It was beautiful in a gothic way. I headed for the only light on in the house, with the smell of coffee wafting in the air.

"I'll be down soon," Jack said from somewhere upstairs, making me flinch. I narrowed my eyes but couldn't see where he was. "Come inside and make yourself at home. Coffee is brewing in the kitchen. Help yourself when it's done."

"Thanks," I said, setting my bag on the table that stood in the center of the neat kitchen. The counter was clean, with a cloth neatly draped over the side of the sink. I reached for one mug and poured myself a cup of coffee after it finished percolating. Unsure where to go, I sat at the antique wooden kitchen table and waited for him.

I glanced around the neat kitchen, at the glass jar of cookies, and imagined a naughty Jack stealing a few before dinner.

"Here," Jack said, entering the kitchen with two pillows and a blanket. "I'll leave these in the second bedroom for you. When you're done with your coffee, you're welcome to freshen up in the bathroom."

"Thanks, I appreciate the help."

"Any time," he said, leaving me alone in the kitchen. He returned, still smiling, and poured himself a cup of coffee and sat across from me.

"Nice place," I started, "well, that which I've seen so far."

"Thanks. It's been in the family for generations."

"It reminds me of those plantation houses."

"Yeah, my great-grandfather came from Louisiana," he said, clearing his throat. "He loved the design of those houses and wanted one here."

"It's lovely." I thought for a moment, then something came to mind. "This is the only plantation-looking house in Ketchum, isn't it?"

"Yes," he said, nodding. He sipped from his coffee, watching me intently.

"Not sure if it's your house," I said, thinking, "but I'd heard a horrific story of a couple murdered during a home invasion in a plantation type of farmhouse around here many years ago."

"Yeah," he said sadly. "They murdered my parents, and they almost killed me." He thumbed behind him. "Stabbed me in my back, hit my head." He pointed at the right-hand side of his temple. "And that's why I don't use the upstairs area anymore. The only time I go up there is to fetch something out of storage."

"I'm sorry," I said, feeling guilty for bringing it up. "I can only imagine how terrible it must've been."

"The cops never caught them, but I hoped they would return so that I could end them myself."

"If you don't mind me asking. How old were you when it happened?"

"Twenty-one."

"No matter what age, it's a terrible thing to experience."

Comfortable silence stretched between us as we sipped our coffee and stared at each other.

"Has anything like that happened to you before?"

I fidgeted with my fingers and nodded. I found it strange yet comforting to have met someone who had gone through something similarly as I had. It was devastating and cruel, but in some strange, twisted fate, Jack and I had something to bond over.

"My real parents were murdered during a home invasion. Luckily, I was with friends when it happened. They stole all my mom's jewelry and tried to sell it. The pawn shop owner called the police and they were arrested."

"I'm sorry, too," Jack said, reaching out to pat my hand. "How old were you?"

"I was thirteen. My aunt adopted me, and we moved here, but for the last two years, she's hardly been home." My aunt sacrificed her love life to give me a comfortable, safe, and stable home. Then, when I was old enough to look after myself, she started dating again. I was happy for her, albeit lonely, but I would forever be grateful for her sacrifices.

"I was old enough to look after myself," he said, licking his lips. "Enough of this sad talk. Are you hungry?

I feel like having a snack. I think I still have pecan pie left over."

"No thank you," I said, as my stomach grumbled.

Jack smiled. "Are you sure?" He offered and stood up. He opened the fridge and pulled out a plate with two slices of pecan pie left.

My stomach grumbled again.

He offered me a fork, and I took it from him with the biggest smile on my face, then our fingers grazed. In that millisecond, we stared at each other, sharing a moment. A moment that bonded us together about losing our parents so violently and making us orphans. It was morbid, but it was still our quiet moment in a world filled with chaos.

He smiled nervously, set the plate between us, and sat down. "Enjoy," he said with a mouthful of pecan pie.

I enjoyed a bite, and it melted in my mouth. "This is delicious. Where did you buy it from?"

"I made it myself. It was my mother's specialty," he said, humming as he chewed.

We ate our slice in silence, then when we finished the pie and our coffee, Jack stood up and cleared the table. I joined him at the sink and helped to wash and rinse the items. For a fleeting moment, our elbows touched, and I felt something spark. I glanced up, and he was staring at me; no doubt he had felt it, too. My heart raced in my chest as heat crept up my neck. He placed his mug on the drying rack and turned to face me.

I set my clean mug beside his. I had to reach around him and again, our bodies touched. Then I glanced up at him again and we just stared at each other. Neither of us moved to go wash up and sleep. We just stood there and stared at one another.

Jack had fine lines near his blue eyes, a light scar above

his lip, and his tanned skin told me he worked outside in the sun often. His hands were powerful, and he kept his nails short. He also kept his dark hair short but neat. His body was muscular yet lean. He seemed like someone who took pride in his physique and kept to a routine.

Then he took me by surprise when he leaned forward and cupped my face. I couldn't resist him; I didn't want to. My lips parted. My eyes closed, and I waited. He leaned closer, kissing me gently; it was a kiss that held so much emotion, which was too soon since we barely knew each other. I guessed it was the bond over the trauma we'd experienced when they murdered our parents.

He let go of my face, reached for my hand and I walked beside him to his bedroom…

Chapter Thirteen

THE ITCH

Jacob - 21 years old
1987

"Hey, Jacob," Katie said with a broad smile. "How's farm life today?" She slammed the door of her Mini Cooper and approached.

I shoveled the last of the manure into the drum and closed it. She got to me as I pulled off my gloves.

"Hey yourself, stranger. How's the diner?" I asked, pulling her in for a hug.

"Eww, you smell like shit." She pushed away from me, her smile fading fast. She dusted imaginary sand off her silk blouse.

"I was just shoveling the stuff." I opened the tap near the new barn and washed my hands at the outside basin so that I was half clean by the time I finished up and went inside the house. "What are you doing here? It's not Sunday."

"I know," she said, glancing away. "But I thought we could move our weekly get together to today because I'm going away the weekend."

My wet hands dropped to my sides as that familiar coldness spread throughout my body. I scratched my neck and flinched when I tore open the scab. I rubbed gently, easing the frustrating pain.

"Which friends are going with you?" I asked calmly.

"Oh you, know."

"No, I don't know. Your friends keep changing as often as I change underwear."

"Jacob," she said, frowning, "that's not nice."

I folded my arms across my chest, waiting for her answer.

"You're still my friend," she said, smiling and tugging on my shirtsleeve. "Is it bleeding again?" She leaned her hand on my shoulder and rocked onto her toes to see the wound at the back of my neck. "Do you have ointment and I'll put some on?"

"I'll be fine," I said, grabbing her wrist and gently removing her arm from my body, and stepped farther away.

She frowned. "Don't be like that, Jacob. I only want to help."

I exhaled an irritated breath and reached for her hand. "Come, let's see what Mama has made for lunch."

"Oh, I hope it's her soup and dumplings."

My mom's favorite dish was a creamy vegetable soup she made which she simmered with dumplings. It was also Katie's favorite, so Mama only made it every Sunday because that's when Katie visited. But today was Thursday, which meant pork chops, mash and steamed veggies, Katie's least favorite meal.

Mama cried out in surprise when Katie entered the

kitchen. "My darling, child. What are you doing here? It's not Sunday," she said. When I walked in behind Katie, Mama glared at me. "You didn't tell me she was coming today, Jacob. She doesn't like pork chops."

"It's okay Aunty Moira, I surprised Jacob. Please don't fret over me." Katie patted Mama's hand, then gave her a hug.

"You're such a darling child," Mama cooed over Katie.

"Katie," Papa said, entering the kitchen. "Jacob never mentioned you would come over today." He glowered at me. "You know your mother enjoys preparing Katie's favorite meal when she visits us."

"It wasn't his fault, Uncle Bill," Katie said, hugging him quickly to shush him, then sat down. "I can only stay for a short while and then I must get back to the diner."

"How is Big John?" Papa asked, sitting at the head of the table.

"He's good. The cast came off his arm yesterday, and he's giving me a raise for all my hard work." Katie beamed.

"That's excellent," Papa said, nodding. "Maybe that will teach Big John not to wrestle with his dog."

"It was an accident, dear," Mama said, placing Papa's plate in front of him. She waited beside him while he had a bite and then nodded. Then she placed our full plates in front of us.

"How is your mother?" Mama asked.

"She's fine," Katie said, not elaborating.

"Is she still dating that sheriff?" Papa asked.

"Yeah," she said. "He makes her happy, and that's all that counts." She didn't sound convincing, but I knew what she really thought of him. "This is lovely, Aunty Moira," Katie said, scooping some mash into her mouth.

For the rest of the meal, we spoke about Big John's dog

kennel and the diner he inherited from his parents. He had asked Katie to manage the staff when he wasn't there and provided her with a generous salary increase.

After lunch, I walked her down the driveway toward her Mini Cooper. She opened the car door but didn't climb inside. She stared at me as if she wanted to say something, pursed her lips, and climbed inside.

"I'll see you next week Sunday," she said, starting the engine.

"Where are you going this weekend?"

"To my mom's cabin," she said, putting the car into first gear. After Katie's father passed away, her mother inherited a couple of millions from his life insurance, and one of her purchases was a cabin in the woods a ten-minute drive from here.

"Can I come with?" I asked, standing closer.

"There aren't enough rooms. Maybe we can go next weekend." She smiled nervously.

"Yeah," I said, pushing her door closed, "sure. Next weekend should be fine. I'm sure my father would give me the weekend off." I doubted my father would, but I could ask.

"Great," she added and started reversing. "I'll let you know if it's possible for next weekend. My mom said they might go."

"Yeah, sure," I said in a monotone, and waved as she drove away. The itch at the back of my neck started up again, and I scratched hard. The scab came loose, and a wetness dripped down between my shoulder blades. "Yeah," I said to myself, "I think I'll see you at the cabin this weekend rather."

Chapter Fourteen

THE NEXT MORNING

Michelle
2002

The sun shining through the curtains and on my face woke me. I blinked, forgetting where I was for a second. Groaning inwardly, I suddenly felt embarrassed about sleeping with someone I'd only just met. I sat up, pulling the duvet tight against my body, relieved Jack was nowhere to be seen.

"You're up," Jack said, peering around the doorjamb.

"Hi, morning," I said, my cheeks heating.

Jack entered the room holding neatly folded clothing. "Here, I thought you might prefer wearing fresh clothes after your shower. No underwear, I'm afraid, but this should do just fine." He placed the clothing on the bed.

"Thanks. Who did it belong to?" I asked, feeling nervous.

"An old girlfriend. She left some of her items here." He shrugged. "Can't please everyone." He scratched the back of his neck. "I'm just outside if you need anything. My friend came over and is looking at your car as we speak. You're welcome to have a shower and then join us when you're done."

"Oh wow, thank you so much." My smile reached my eyes. "It's not often people go out of their way to help someone they only met hours ago."

"The world needs more kind, helpful people." He smacked the doorjamb for effect, then added, "Your car should be sorted by the time you're ready."

"Ok," I said, beaming up at him. When he left, I scooted off the bed, pulled the blanket around my body, scooped up the fresh clothing, reached for my handbag, and entered the bathroom.

I flicked the light on and shielded my eyes; everything was bright white, and the white light made everything that much brighter. Being a nosy person, I opened the medicine cabinet; shaving gel, floss, toothpaste, men's aftershave. Then right at the top were orange child-proof medicine bottles; Thorazine, Vicodin, and Lithobid. It concerned me they had prescribed this kind of medication for a child. But what struck me as odd was the medication was very old, from 1980, and I wondered why Jack kept it and why he never mentioned having a brother named Jacob. I chalked it up to us not knowing each other very well and put the bottles back where I found them.

I used the toilet and had a quick, hot shower, filling the bathroom with steam. There was only one towel hanging up which I used and pulled on the clothing without looking at it first. The t-shirt and jeans fit perfectly. I wiped the mirror with the towel but every time I did that, it fogged up again; obviously my shower was hotter than I thought. I placed my dirty clothing inside my handbag, grabbed the small floral perfume bottle and spritzed some on my neck and wrists. I saw my gun, relieved it was still in my bag even though I didn't need to use it, and slung the strap over my shoulder.

I placed the blanket that I'd wrapped around my body on the bed, pulled on my coat, and headed outside. When I reached the mirror by the front door, I glanced at myself quickly and blood drained from my face. My limbs went cold, and my fight-or-flight instincts kicked in. I looked outside and Jack was speaking with a man near my car; the hood was open, and they were pointing at the battery.

I turned to look at the shirt I had bought Jessica, the one with The Rolling Stones' tongue and lips, and I had to be wrong. This was a common shirt. It couldn't have been a coincidence that the man who had taken her had helped me. Was it? But I knew this shirt was Jessica's.

She had left with a well-known resident of Ketchum.

A man everybody knew.

A man charming enough to help me, then offer me a ride home.

A man who knew how to manipulate women.

A man who slept with and kidnapped women.

My stomach twisted and turned. I reached for the wall to keep myself from falling over.

"Michelle," Jack called, "He fixed your car."

The other man was in my car and started the engine. It relieved me that my car worked, and I could get out of here. I could tell that detective what I'd discovered, and he could bring everyone here to arrest this man. But I first needed to find Jessica. I was already here, and I would never forgive myself if I could save her from that man. She had to be here somewhere. All I had to do was find her.

"Michelle," Jack yelled again, waving me over.

I swallowed hard as I approached Jack. No matter what

I did, I had to play it cool, or he'd become suspicious. But in my head, all I thought about was finding Jessica.

Jack called again.

Slowly, I pushed the front screen door open. I fisted my left hand while gripping the strap of my bag with my right. I needed easy access to my gun if Jack provoked me.

"She's all fixed," Jack said, rubbing my back.

"Thank you so much," I said, smiling, but it didn't reach my eyes. "How much do I owe you?"

"Nothing, miss," said the man sitting in my driver's seat. "Jack's paying."

"Thank you," I said, staring at Jack.

"My pleasure." There was something in his expression I couldn't decipher. It was like the same look from last night, and I suddenly felt like prey and needed to get out of here. No, not yet. I had to look for Jessica upstairs and then in his basement.

"Is it all right if I use the bathroom before I leave?"

"Sure," Jack said, still rubbing my back, "I'll be out here if you need me."

I left the men and headed for the house. All the way walking up the path toward his farmhouse, I could feel his dark gaze on my back. I didn't want to turn around and look at him, otherwise he'd see my nervousness, but I felt him.

I hurried inside the house, the screen door slamming behind me, and headed for the bathroom. I glanced over my shoulder and Jack was chatting with the man, giving me an opportunity to check upstairs quickly.

The balustrade had a thick layer of dust, and as I climbed the creaky stairs, dread filled my body. When I reached the top, I saw nothing but darkness and cursed myself for not having a flashlight.

The smell of mold caught me off guard, but I kept thinking I had to find Jessica. She was here. "Jessica?" I called in a soft whisper. I didn't want Jack hearing me call her name. "Jessica, are you here?"

Once my eyes adjusted to the darkness, I made out the first door and headed in that direction. I turned the doorknob, but found it locked.

Men's voices became louder as they approached the house.

As much as I wanted to check the other two rooms, I had to get downstairs. I hurried down the stairs and darted for the bathroom before they entered the house. I washed my hands, flushed the toilet, opened the bathroom door and almost walked into Jack. He was no longer smiling.

"Coffee?" he asked, plastering on a fake smile.

"Uh, sure," I said, hesitating. Something told me he knew what I was up to. Although I wanted to find Jessica, the best thing for me right now was to leave and call the cops. We could come back here and search his house for Jessica then. As much as I wanted to find my friend now, I wouldn't be able to. It was too dangerous.

"You know," I said uneasily, "on second thought perhaps I should go." I headed for the front door, but Jack grabbed my hand and pulled me along with him toward the kitchen.

"First meet Kevin," Jack said, introducing us. "He's my go-to-guy for anything car related. He helped restore my Corvette."

"Hi," I said, shaking his hand. "Nice to meet you." I wiped my hand on my pants.

"Same, darlin'," Kevin said, wiping his dirty hands on his overall. When he smiled I noted a deep scar running from his upper lip to his nose. The stubble on his jaw didn't hide the other scar that ran from his left ear and under his jaw. I wondered whether he had been in an accident.

"Thanks for the coffee, Jack, but I must be on my way. Goodbye, miss," Kevin said, tipping an imaginary hat in my direction. He smiled as he passed me, and his features softened but there was something else there that I assumed was pity.

I watched Kevin leave like he was my only lifeline. All I had to do was call out to him, to tell him to wait for me, but I froze. I closed my mouth as if an imaginary force had silenced me, my dark eyes widening with fear.

Jack closed the front door after Kevin left and turned to face me. His lips twisted in an unfriendly smile, with a cunning glint in his eyes. His demeanor was devoid of the warmth and care I'd felt last night.

I headed for the front door. "Thanks for everything," I said as calmly as possible. "But I need to go home now." I reached for the front door when Jack shoved my head into the mirror. My head hit the object hard, it crashed to the floor, and it shattered, then Jack caught me before I joined the broken shards on the ground.

"Sorry, Michelle, but you aren't going anywhere."

Chapter Fifteen

THE CABIN

Jacob
1987

Mama and Papa were asleep by eight as usual, and I borrowed the car to drive the ten minutes to Katie's cabin. I parked the car between two large, leafy trees, which created enough camouflage that I doubted anyone could see the car from the ID-75 into Ketchum.

I glanced at the box on the seat beside me. I'd saved the hundred dollars to buy Katie the ruby ring she'd always wanted; a silver ring with a red oval halo ruby. It would look stunning on her delicate ring finger. She reminded me of someone who played piano; she had long fingers that could dance across the black and white keys if she played. But she didn't. The only thing she played with was my heart strings.

Ever since that day in the barn, I couldn't get her out of my mind. I'd known since then that she would be mine in all ways. But as the years progressed, we always just remained friends. Katie would go off with her other friends without me. She knew I wouldn't get on with the others; I was far too mature for them; she had said one day. But in the end, she tried to make time for me.

I loved the moments when it was just the two of us. We would share an ice cream, walked hand in hand some days, and sometimes she would sit in my lap while hugging me. It was our very own special bond; just us versus the world.

I flinched when a car sped past. The tires squealed as they turned the corner. It wasn't Katie's Mini Cooper, but the latest BMW.

I sat upright, wiping sleep from my eyes. As they drove past, rock music blared, ruining the peaceful atmosphere. I glimpsed Katie's beautiful face. Her smiled captivated me, but the itch at the back of my neck brought me back to the reason I was there.

Narrowing my eyes, I snatched the box from the seat and opened the car door. Traversing through the rough terrain calmed me enough so that by the time I arrived at the cabin I was relaxed, but the itch remained.

The cabin Katie's mom had bought soon after her father had died was one of those double story minimansions that enjoyed scenic views of the trees surrounding them with open waters of a river as their front yard. It was stunning. When Katie first told me about it, I couldn't wait to see it, but she had never brought me here. In all the years since her father's death, not once had she offered to bring me here.

My hands fisted again when I realized it was just her and some man. There wasn't a group of friends, it was just the two of them; she lied... again. I did those breathing techniques that helped panic attack sufferers, and my anger slowly subsided. There were things I needed to do and losing my cool now wasn't going to help me accomplish anything.

I huffed as I pushed through thick terrain, my shoes crunching on loose ground and leaves. The air smelled wet and cold, as if rain threatened in the distance, with the delicate tweeting of birds above me in trees.

He parked the BMW out front and left the trunk open. They were upstairs somewhere, laughing. I rolled my eyes and peered inside the trunk, opening the only suitcase there; it belonged to him. I rummaged through his items and zipped it once more. Their voices travelled down the stairs and toward the front door, while I traversed along the side of the house, out of view.

"I can't wait to get you naked," the man said in a low growl that dripped with sex.

I stopped to listen and glanced over my shoulder. Unable to see them, but I heard their kissing sounds. I slammed my fist into the wall, scraping my knuckles. My jaw ticked at the things this man was doing to my Katie but knew that he would get what was coming to him.

I licked the blood from my knuckles, savoring the metallic taste in my mouth, and followed the path to the other side of the house. There was a small splash pool and deck, with a barbecue and pizza oven section on one side; another detail Katie had forgotten to mention.

I peered through the glass and the furniture in the living room was of items I'd only seen on television and fashion magazines. It angered me that Katie had never once mentioned this. What made it worse was why had she never brought me here.

The more I thought about it, I realized she never invited me to her home in Ketchum, either. I'd always left her at her front door, or she would meet me at the venue. No, there was that one time when we first met, she had invited me in, but then never again.

I shook my head in disappointment. Things could've been different between us, but she had been keeping many things from me. Too many things. While I stood around in the shadows, being her friend only when she needed me, only when she wanted me. I felt like discarded trash she kept taking out and using only when she felt like it.

Never again.

Stomping across the manicured lawn between trees, I wondered how often the gardeners tended to it. Unless they had a caretaker looking after the place when they weren't here, and he fixed things up for them before their arrival.

I headed for the jetty and boathouse. Another item she had forgotten to tell me. The door creaked open. I pushed the door wider and whistled when my eyes found the large boat under a cover. I peeked at the boat, and it looked new.

The rest of the boathouse had shelves on one side and the various tools one would use to maintain a house. They even kept the lawnmower and garden hedge shears here.

Again, everything I had discovered now at her cabin had caught me off guard. Katie hadn't told me about most of the stuff and I wondered what else hadn't she told me. But I'd find out soon enough.

Loud voices sounded, and they were heading in this direction. I needed to find a hiding spot, but there were none. It was a wooden shack over water with no closets or lockers, and only one way in or out; either through the water or back the way I came.

The voices grew louder as they neared.

The boat rocked back and forth from the water splashing against the sides.

The footsteps neared.

I moved toward the boat.

The door opened.

I eased into the dark water.

Katie giggled; it was a sound I'd never heard before. My frown deepened at the thought of not knowing who Katie really was; she was my best friend, my lover, the love of my life. Yet, I knew nothing about her. That didn't matter. We had the rest of our lives to get to know one another.

The cold water stole my breath as I sunk deeper and moved to the other side of the boat and away from the kissing couple.

I waded quietly in the water and moved to the front of the boat and under the deck so that if they took the boat out for an evening drive, they wouldn't see me.

The boat rocked as they climbed into it. The water lapped harder against the sides of the boat as their laughter, kissing, and groping intensified.

I held onto the deck and waited.

The quiet evening pierced my ears. Carefully, I climbed out of the water and onto the wooden deck without making a sound. I exhaled silently as I monitored the couple fast asleep in the boat. Tiptoeing on the wooden deck, I was careful not to stand on a creaking plank and when I reached the door, Katie stirred in the boat, mumbling someone's name. I opened the door, testing to ensure it didn't moan the wider I opened it, and slipped out.

I traversed the dark path to the house and entered. Leaving the lights off, I navigated my way around the living room, kitchen, until finally upstairs. I entered the main bedroom and found his suitcase again. Flipping through his wallet, I found what I was looking for and headed back down to the kitchen. Their food remained on the counter, waiting for them to enjoy, and I opened the pantry door.

Once done, I slipped out the front door and found a place hidden in shadows where I could see most of the house and waited. I heard cars driving on the ID-75 entering and exiting Ketchum and was grateful they were a distance away and wouldn't see me or my vehicle from the road.

It was ten at night by the time Katie and her friend staggered up the path, switching on lights as they entered the house and headed for the kitchen. Katie warmed their dinner while her friend sat at the table, waiting for her to serve him.

The itch at the back of my neck started up again, but I didn't scratch. Instead, I just rubbed the offending area and waited patiently.

Katie dished food onto their plates and sat beside him. My body heated as I watched him eat. All was fine for a few seconds and then… he grabbed his throat. His eyes widened in horror. Red blotches formed on his face and neck. His face started swelling, along with one side of his neck. He pushed away from the table, stood up, then doubled over as if trying to expel whatever was lodged in his throat. Katie was there to slap him on his back, but nothing helped.

Nothing would help him.

The man pointed to the stairs and then to his neck. Katie nodded and frantically ran upstairs.

Moments later, she returned, shaking her head. "There's nothing there," she cried.

Shock flashed in his eyes. He collapsed onto his knees, then fell on his chest and face, unmoving.

Katie dashed around, looking for something, but there was nothing that could help him. She fell to her knees and moved him onto his back so she could proceed with CPR, but his throat had already closed, shutting off all his air supply.

From where I stood, his face and neck had swollen to the point where his cheeks were red, round and puffy, and his eyes had bulged. While his fat lips had started turning purple.

After about ten minutes, Katie sat back on her haunches, crying into her hands.

I dropped the epinephrine injection on the ground and crushed it with my boot heel. Pushing through the branches, I approached the cabin with purpose and entered through the front door.

Katie flinched when she saw me and stood up. "Jacob, what are you doing here?" she asked, glancing nervously at me and then at her friend on the floor.

"I thought you might need some help," I said mysteriously and crossed the threshold. My clothing was still damp, and I left wet marks everywhere I stepped.

Katie backed up, glancing at me and the body. "We need to call for help," she stammered, "could you—"

"No," I yelled, shutting her up. "No more, Katie," I snapped. "You've been playing me for years. No more." I pulled the box out of my pocket and placed it gently on the counter. "I've had this for about a year, waiting for the right time to give it to you. To ask for your hand in marriage. Ever since that day in the barn, I've loved you more than anything else. I would've given you the world, anything, and everything you ever wanted. But," I paused for effect and stared into her sad, blue eyes, "you've made it perfectly clear where I stand with you."

Katie's eyes welled with tears. "I'm sorry you feel that way. I didn't mean to hurt you, Jacob. In my eyes, we were only friends. We are best friends, and to me that's better than a boyfriend I would never marry. Don't you understand, I'm never going to marry anyone. I saw what my mom did to my dad. I would never do that to anyone I loved. And you're my best friend, Jacob. I love you in my own special way."

"That's enough." My tone was void of emotion as my heart thundered in my chest. "Did you ever love me, or are you just saying that to make me happy?"

She swallowed hard. Her eyes flicked from the body on the floor to me. I was sure she assumed I caused his demise.

"Answer me," I demanded, making her flinch.

"Yes, I truly love you… but the way a sister loves her brother."

I cocked my head to the side, staring at her. My dark gaze made her uncomfortable. Her pale skin was slowly returning to normal, and her cheeks were almost pink, like they usually were. Her full lips were their usual red color, while her features were still as delicate as a wilting flower.

But her eyes; they were the color of ice glaciers, and the dark shadows she had used to color in her face ruined her innocent features.

"Since when do you wear so much makeup?" I asked, stepping closer to inspect the mess on her face.

"I always wear makeup," she said, stepping away.

"Never this much, Katie," I said, my tone harsh.

She stared at me, unmoving.

"Was I your first? That day in the barn. Was it your first time, too?"

She averted her eyes.

A rush of adrenaline flooded my system.

"Was I your first?" I yelled.

"No," she blurted, crying. "No," she whispered.

"We were sixteen. How many others were there before me?" I closed the gap, cornering her between the two kitchen counters.

"About three."

"About three, or maybe more?"

"Four, okay, there were four guys before you," she said, choking on her sob.

I stood back and glowered down at her. "When did you become a slut?"

She pursed her lips. "I'm not a slut. A man can sleep with whomever he wants, and it's fine. The moment a woman becomes active and does the same, she's a slut."

"Answer me," I growled. "When did you become active?"

The muscles near her jaw ticked a little, and she fisted her hands. I'd never seen her this angry before. "That year," she finally said.

I stood back, scowling at her. "You slept with five guys in one year." I shook my head. My heart squeezing at the thought of another man touching her soft skin… before I ever had the chance. Tears welled in my eyes, but I blinked them away.

"I enjoy having sex and you want to make me feel bad about it. Go to hell, Jacob!"

"No!" I said, my tone deep and throaty. "It's not fair. You hid it from me, you lied, and you avoided me. You kept me on one side, and always made excuses not to meet at a cafe or restaurant like you were too embarrassed to be around me. We always ate at my parent's house. You led me on."

"No," she shook her head, "I never led you on. I always told you we were good friends. That we were only friends."

I fisted my hands and exhaled slowly. It didn't matter what she said, she would lie. She lied about everything and would continue to spin any tale to get out of the corner she put herself in.

I decided then that no woman would ever hurt me like this again. My heart would never bleed for another woman again. And I would take what was mine.

"I only ever showed you love and compassion," I said through gritted teeth. "And this is how you treat me."

I lunged and hit her in the face, catching her before she crashed to the floor.

Chapter Sixteen

GET OUT

Michelle
2002

My head ached.

My body trembled.

I groaned as I reached to wipe the liquid from my eyes. Then I moved and there was pressure on my abdomen and blood rushed to my head, followed by more liquid pouring into my face.

"I must say, you look ravishing in Jessica's clothing," Jack said in a sinister tone. "If only you were as light as her, though." He groaned as he adjusted me on his shoulder so that he was comfortable, but the pain in my abdomen intensified along with my throbbing head.

"Ah," I said, pushing my elbows against his back so that the pressure lessened.

"There, there, you'll be home soon." Jack smacked my bum, then stepped down, and although I couldn't open my eyes, I sensed darkness behind my eyelids. "You can be glad I still have space. Man, if I'd known you'd fall into my lap the way you did, I would've made your new accommodations a bit comfier. Anyway, it will have to do." He continued stepping down until he reached a flat surface.

The smell of chemicals and dirt wafted in the air, and I imagined we were in his basement.

Hair tickled my face, my reactions were slow, and the moment I moved hair out of my face, pain shot up my spine, neck, and head.

I wiped the dry blood out of my eyes without causing more pain, and I could finally see where we were. There was dark sand below us. Behind us, metal doors with a bright light growing smaller as we traversed deeper into the bowels of an underground level.

"Here we go," he said. Wood creaked and slammed against something. He stepped down again and the smell of stale, wet sand filled my lungs and I wheezed. "Get used to it, darling. This is your new home."

I tried to see where we were, but he'd entered a small room and all I saw was the wooden door across from me.

"This is all yours, Michelle," Jack said, kicking something.

Without warning, he flipped me off his shoulder. My legs collapsed beneath me and I crashed to the hard dirt below. I winced once more and moved onto my side. There was pain on my left-hand side I hadn't felt before, but the more I leaned on that side, the worse it got. I was grateful my right-hand side still felt ok.

"Right," Jack said in a serious tone. "If you want to live, there are a few rules you need to abide by." He paused for effect. I glanced up at him, but he was blurry around the edges. "Rule number one, you will never get out of here, so don't bother screaming for help or calling out to your neighbors. They know the rules and they'll never break them. Rule number two, don't fight me, ever. And lastly, when I come into your room, you will do as I say! Do you hear me?"

I nodded.

"Good. Now I must go fetch something, so wait here quietly until I come back." With his parting words, he slammed the wooden door shut and locked it.

I leaned back in the dark dirt, my fingers digging into the hard, cold sand. My eyes adjusted to the darkness, but there's nothing much to see.

Dread filled me when I realized he was going to kill me. I was sure of it. Or he would keep me here, starve me, then possibly eat me and dress himself in my skin. I shuddered at the thought.

A tear slid down my face and I wiped it away with the back of my hand. No, I couldn't allow this man to do any of that to me. I had to find a way out of here.

I climbed onto my hands and knees, was careful not to aggravate the tender limbs, and crawled around the area looking for something, anything, to help me get out of here.

On my left was the door he'd just closed, and although I'd heard him lock it, I tried the handle anyway, but it didn't budge. Then I followed along the sides of my enclosure and then I flinched when I touched something soft.

"Hello?" I whispered as I continued feeling with my fingertips. It felt like a thin mattress. The closer I came to it, the more I smelled urine and gagged. I yanked the mattress to the other side and could breathe again.

I continued feeling my way across the damp dirt and the walls. There were tiny stones and some loose dirt. Perhaps I could dig my way out, and I started scooping the loose sand away. I was near the back end of the room, hoping to find a way out, but as I dug out the sand, I became less convinced that it would lead to freedom.

I winced when my fingers grazed against something solid. I dug my fingernails deeper into the dirt, curling them around the object; it took some wiggling, but I finally got it loose and pulled it out.

Unable to see much apart from the outline of the object and from what I could feel, it was a small gardening spade. I sighed with relief; I had a weapon. It was small, but it was something I could use against him. The spade's handle was wooden and the spade part metal. It was heavy and sharp enough to cause damage. My only hope was I had enough energy and force to use it on him.

Now that I had a weapon I could sit and breathe for a moment. With my head against the wooden wall, my legs stretched out in front of me, the weapon in both hands, I listened as I steadied my breathing. There was no sound from anywhere; beside me or upstairs. I imagined the walls for each of these rooms were solid and provided structural support for the rest of the house, but I needed to find out if there was anyone else down here.

"Hello!" I called.

Nothing.

"Anyone out there?"

Silence.

"Jessica?"

The soundless darkness weighed on me.

I bit my lip as I waited for Jack's return, clutching the spade tightly against my chest. My breathing steadied as I listened to the heavy silence around me. The thick darkness enveloped me as the noiseless shadows made me feel deaf and blind. All I heard and felt was my heart thumping inside of my chest.

For a moment, I closed my eyes and listened.

Nothing.

My heart beat rapidly against my chest.

My pulse steadied.

Furniture scraped across the floor and my eyes shot open.

My heart rate kicked up a notch.

I twisted the spade between my hands until it hurt.

Jack stomped across the floor upstairs and slammed a door.

I stood up, feeling my way around my enclosure. My left-hand side still ached, but I pushed the pain away; I would deal with it once I was out of this place.

Metal creaked, and I hurried to the other side of the room.

Footsteps neared.

The lock turned and clicked. The door handle creaked as it twisted down. A dark figure entered the room and as he turned around, I slammed the spade into his head over and over until a wetness hit me in the face and he fell to the ground.

I bolted out of my enclosure, closed the door behind me, but forgot to get the keys from his hand. I didn't have time to go back in. Just now, he got up and came after me again. All I needed in that moment was to get out of his house of horrors.

I ran for the only light down here, bursting through the metal doors and they clanked against the sides. I sprinted up the basement stairs; two at a time, through the kitchen, grabbed any sharp knife from the table in case he advanced on me again, and out the front door. Then I remembered something, and I went back inside, grabbed my bag that was still on the floor, found my car keys beside them, and ran out again.

My hand shook as I tried to get the key in the ignition.

Condensation filled my vision as I wheezed.

Snow fell around me.

Wind howled outside.

Every time I glanced up at his house, it relieved me I saw nobody.

When I finally inserted the key, I turned it, and the car roared to life. I pulled my door closed and smashed the gas, speeding the hell out of there.

"Jesus, Michelle, what happened to you?" Mike asked when I burst through his front door. His mother dropped her water glass and shrieked. Their dog, Bingo, barked, and Mike almost jumped on top of me.

"You won't believe it, Mike. You won't believe who I found," I said. My hands shaking as I removed my bag from my wounded shoulder and pulled on Jessica's t-shirt. "It's Jessica's," I whispered. "The asshole gave me Jessica's shirt to wear. He knew I was looking for her."

"Hold up," Mike said, staring at the t-shirt. "Tell me everything that happened? How?" He raised his hands, his face screaming confusion.

I grabbed Mike's hand and pulled him toward the living area. I apologized to his mom for my outburst, rubbed the dog's head, and sat on the couch and winced. Then, while his mom made us coffee, I explained everything that had happened to me.

The Last Girl

"Let me get the first aid kit," Mike said, pointing at my shoulder. "You're bleeding everywhere."

"What?" I said, glancing behind me and saw the blood on the couch. "Sorry," I said, cringing.

Mike returned with the items he needed and helped me out of my jacket and Jessica's t-shirt. There were shards of glass lodged in my skin near my shoulder, with a few cuts on the side of my face and a big bump. I was relieved my swollen eye had no permanent damage.

Mike's mom gave us our coffee with a tray filled with cheese scones. I thanked her and sipped on the coffee. My hands shook, almost spilling the contents all over my lap.

I sucked in deep breaths and wanted to cry each time.

"Let me take you to the police station so you can tell the detective everything you told me now."

That made sense. Then the detective could go to Jack's house and arrest him. But then I remembered how they had handled Jessica's case and had given up on her after a few days. They didn't bother searching for her. Yet I was the one who found her kidnapper.

"Sure, you could take me there. But—" I left my word hanging.

Mike narrowed his eyes at me. "But what, Michelle?"

"I want to go back there and look for her myself."

Mike shook his head. "You're crazy. There's no way he'll let you go free again. He'll catch you and kill you."

I shrugged. "She's my friend. She would do the same. I don't trust the police, Mike. I need to be the one who rescues her."

"No, you don't," he said, unhappy. "It won't end well."

I stared hard into his eyes. "I'll phone the detective the moment I arrive at Jack's house so that when they come looking for me, he won't have time to do anything to me."

As I said the words, I kept thinking about being in bed with Jack. I couldn't believe I slept with him; I was so stupid. That's the other reason I wanted to be alone with him one last time. I wanted him to know what he did to me was wrong. He had known I was Jessica's friend, yet he still slept with me; using our tragic history for us to bond over. I shuddered at the thought. I wanted to hurt him so badly.

My plan was solid. I would dump my vehicle somewhere for the police to find, leave Jessica's top, add some of my blood, the knife I'd taken from Jack's house, along with some of my hair. I searched for the items in my handbag and realized my gun was missing, and ice filled my veins; he had my gun. All the more reason to return and retrieve it. It was a gun given to me by a friend of a friend and they had removed the serial number. If the police found this, my other friend would get into trouble.

I shook my head in disappointment; how could I be so stupid? I needed to focus on the plan. We could remove the plates from the car, make the police work a little, make it look real. I didn't want them thinking it was easy. It didn't have to make sense, but it had to look like Jack had dumped my car somewhere. And then I would enter his house and rescue Jessica.

After what felt like hours sitting on Mike's couch concocting this plan and sharing what had happened last night, a tiredness settled into my bones, one I'd never felt before, and I just wanted to sleep so that this could be over.

Mike said something I didn't hear and I looked at him. "Huh?" I said.

"Nothing. You look exhausted," he said, scooting closer to me. "Come, lie here by me."

Chapter Seventeen

THE FIRST "KEY"

Jacob
1987

My farmhouse came into view, and I killed the headlights, grateful the moon was bright enough for me to see clearly. Taking the car out of gear, I idled my way closer to the basement bulkhead, ensuring I didn't wake my parents. The last thing I needed was my father complaining or my mother seeing Katie in the trunk.

I opened the bulkhead and returned to the car, opening the trunk. Quickly and quietly, I picked Katie up and silently traversed toward the stairs with her safely in my warm arms. She shivered in her slumber, and I carefully moved hair out of her face. Her features in the moonlight brought the protector out of me. I wanted to keep her safe, but I could only do that if she stayed with me.

I maneuvered down the three steps into the basement and through the open metal lockers into the underground area. The smell of wet dirt and stale sweat assaulted my nose, but it didn't bother me. It reminded me of my grandfather. He and I had spent a lot of time together before he passed away.

I had installed the metal lockers with a secret panel so that anyone who came down here didn't know about the second level. It wasn't something Papa enjoyed talking about, and I never pushed for answers. So, when I suggested it, he agreed. Whatever the secret was, Papa was relieved to keep it hidden.

I remembered the secrets granddad told me about our family fortune. But back then, I thought he had lost his mind until I investigated myself. I'd found the safe my father had installed in the wall in his room and used the key I'd found in my mother's underwear drawer to open it. Inside were bars of gold, bonds, diamonds, a will, and bank statements. I couldn't believe my father had lied to me all the years telling me how dirt poor we were, but in the meantime, we had millions in the bank.

Granddad and I used to come down here with our lanterns to see the carvings on the wood left by the builders. I remember asking granddad what each stall was for, and he always patted me on my head and said it was nothing for me to worry about. They had separated each room with hardwood, and they were big enough for a person to sleep in. I assumed it was structural support for the house.

I shifted Katie's body to my other shoulder and entered the first stall.

Before I headed for her cabin, I left a lantern on and a thin mattress on the floor, covered it with an old sheet and one of my cleaner pillows. Carefully, I settled Katie on the mattress. She stirred as she got comfortable, then fell asleep again.

The Last Girl

I stood straight, stretched my back and neck, and relieved the itch no longer bothered me. I stared down at my *First*; my first Trophy, my first Love, my first *Key*.

I pulled the keychain out of my pocket and rubbed the *Key* that would ensure she remained here with me until the end.

I crouched near her, checked her bottle of water and a sandwich wrapped in foil, and leaned forward, kissing her temple. She stirred again, mumbling words I couldn't understand.

I stood again and closed her door behind me, slipping her *Key* inside and turned, locking the door. I placed my hand on the cold wood, the roughness beneath my touch a reminder that life could be cruel, but it could also be kind, and I would give her both.

I would be her captor and savior.

I would also be her lover.

And we would be together forever.

Chapter Eighteen

BLINDSIDED

Jack
2002

I hated I didn't see her blindside me like that. She was quick and had hit me so hard with that... what was it? I stood up slowly, shining my flashlight on the ground, and found the mattress on one side with an old spade I had played with as a kid. I'd forgotten about that thing, remembering the cat I'd killed that day.

Something trickled down my back and between my shoulder blades. I felt the back of my head, my fingers touching something wet along with an egg forming on my head, and a superficial cut. When I shone the flashlight on my red stained fingers, anger flooded my veins, and I slammed my fist into the door, cracking it and hurting my knuckles.

I can't believe that bitch hit me. And she escaped. I thought to myself as the rumbling of her car caught my attention, and then she drove away. But something told me she wouldn't go to the cops. She was bravely trying to search for her friend before I caught her and was sure she would return to be the one who found Jessica. I was sure of it.

I smiled. Yep, that bitch would be back all right, and I knew just what to do when that happened.

I exited the room, and it relieved me she didn't lock the metal doors behind her, otherwise I'd be stuck down here forever. I needed to install a mechanism to open them from this side, but I didn't want any of my *Keys* escaping.

I made a mental note to do that later. There were more important things I needed to do now.

Traversing up the basement stairs, still feeling the egg and wound on my head, and entered the kitchen; everything was as it should be. Michelle had taken her bag and clothing with her, leaving no trace of her behind other than the now broken mirror.

I grabbed the brush and scoop and cleaned the mess, throwing my mother's antique mirror and frame away. I glanced at the spot where the mirror had hung, reminding me how old this place was. The wall had stained an off-yellow color through the years but was white in the mirror's shape. My attention drifted to the upstairs section where good and bad memories lived.

My tummy grumbled. Before I did anything, I would eat.

I boiled one egg, and made one slice of toast. My knife and fork were at its correct spot, with my plate perfectly in the middle. I glanced up at the head of the table, nodded, and ate a quiet breakfast.

The wound at the back of my head had stopped bleeding. I doubted I needed stitches, and it relieved me that there wasn't any other damage.

After breakfast, I enjoyed a warm shower, washed the dirty girl's essence from my skin, and the itch at the back of my neck had stopped bothering me.

I sat at the table again drinking my coffee, thinking. I needed to finalize things in case Michelle came back, or the police knocked on my door.

But first, I needed to see if my *Keys* were doing okay. I was sure Michelle had disturbed them, and it relieved me none of them had cried out for help or had tried to escape.

They all knew the rules.

They always followed my rules.

They were good girls and didn't want to disappoint me.

I took care of them; they were mine as I was theirs.

Chapter Nineteen

KEY #5

Jack
1991

I tended to my lethal garden, removed my gloves, and washed my hands thoroughly. The last thing I needed was to rub my eyes and there was something on my fingers. I was too far from the hospital and even farther from neighbors; nobody could help me even if I tried.

I'd long ago gotten rid of the cattle and sheep my father had kept on the farm. All the years shoveling shit from the chicken coop or adding feed for the livestock had taken its toll on me. I had vowed not to continue with how my father ran things and instead did what I wanted; planted sunflowers. I loved waking up in the mornings and while I drank my coffee, I'd look out of the kitchen window onto a field of pretty yellow flowers.

They brought me as much joy as my *Keys* did.

The back of my neck itched as something downstairs

stirred; my *Keys* were awake, and they were hungry. My lovely, wholesome, *Keys*. I smiled as I grabbed my flashlight, ran down the basement stairs, through the metal locker doors, and stopped to listen who had made a sound.

Silence.

"Which one of you called out?" I said. My tone was so ominous my arms pebble. "Come on," I said, traversing down the dirt corridor. "Which one of you called? Or were you calling for me?" I smiled at the thought. Not one of my *Keys* had ever called for me before. There was always a first time for everything.

Something twitched up ahead, and I closed the gap, shining my flashlight in the sound's direction; a tiny mouse scuttled across the damp soil and into a hole in one of the wooden doors. There were twenty tiny cubicles, big enough for someone to sleep in, with some hooks on each of the walls for their clothing.

I had four beautiful *Keys* at my disposal. Four marvelous *Keys* to do with as I pleased.

Now that I knew the source of the noise, I turned around and headed back out, but not before slowly walking past each of the locked doors. I touched each door with the palm of my hand and whispered *'I love you's'* to each of them.

They each whimpered in response.

"I'll bring some food down for each of you shortly," I shouted. "I have a few chores still to do before lunchtime."

I'd already eaten and had just finished making my *Keys* their lunches when I saw someone walking toward the house.

The Last Girl

Placing the food on the counter, I opened the front door and waited on the wide veranda for her to get to me.

"Good afternoon, sir," she said, out of breath. She had tied her medium, brown-colored hair in a low messy ponytail. She removed her sunglasses to reveal pretty big brown eyes. Her facial features were sharp yet delicate, with skin as fine as porcelain. Her eyes darted between me and the house as she licked her dry lips.

"Good afternoon, long way from home?" I asked, folding my arms across my chest.

"Yes," she said nervously, "just passing through. But to get where I want to go, I need to make some extra cash. And... um... I was hoping you had a job for me?"

"Work you say," I said, licking my salty lips. Sweat beaded down the sides of my face. It was unusually hot this time of year.

"Yes, sir. My name is Olivia," she said, looking me in the eye for the first time.

I proffered a hand, which she shook. Her hands were soft and delicate. My smile reached my eyes. "Jack," I said, "pleasure to meet you."

She tugged on her dirty shirt and swapped the only bag she carried for the other shoulder. Her shoes had seen better days, and her thin shorts were best used as a rag to clean my toilet.

"Well, I'm not one to just hand out jobs to anyone who ventures onto my land. But," I said, pausing for effect, "I need help around the house if you wouldn't mind cleaning?"

"Oh yes, sir, I can cook and clean."

"Good," I said, grinning. "Well, come on in." I opened the screen door. "The bathroom is to the right. I'm sure you're dying to freshen up."

"Thank you, sir. And yes, please, sir. I'd love a shower." She pulled on her dirty shirt.

"Please stop calling me, sir. That was my father's name. Just call me Jack."

"Thank you, Jack. I appreciate your help."

Olivia went to the bathroom to freshen up. She took a good half an hour and when she exited the bathroom; she dressed in fresh clothing, leaving her wet hair loose around her shoulders, and asked if she could wash her clothing. I took her bag of dirty clothing and instructed her to eat the sandwich I'd left for her on the kitchen table.

"You can start cleaning tomorrow," I said when I returned from switching on the washing machine in the basement. "For today, you can relax and get your energy back. You're pale and I'd prefer you not falling over when you need to wash the floors." I smiled, picking up her plate and empty milk glass, placing them in the sink.

"Thank you, that was delicious." She pushed her chair back as quietly as possible, stood up, and lifted the chair when she put it back in place.

"Let me show you around first." I called her over as I opened the back door and stepped down. "I grow sunflowers, but I also have a deadly flower garden over there," I pointed in the distance to a spot beside my sunflower, "which you should never touch," I said, arching an eyebrow. "There is no medicine here and you will die. So, it's best not to go near that garden. Understand?"

"Yes, sir," she said, staring at the sunflowers and then the deadly plants as we passed them.

"I sell the sunflowers after they bloom to the farmers next door." We walked around the farmhouse. "There's a couple of acres of land if you feel like going for a walk, but something tells me you'd rather sleep." We neared the barn.

The Last Girl

The side door was open, and I stood on one side so she could enter first.

"Oh wow, I've never seen a barn so neat before."

I chuckled. "Yeah, there's no hay or straw or horses here." There were shelves lined with jams I'd made that were ready to be shipped off to the market Ketchum hosted once a month. There was a small kitchenette I used to make the jams, with a full-sized bathroom. And upstairs I'd renovated, so that I had an additional bedroom for days I needed to get out of the house a bit.

"It looks like a giant kitchen and loft. Did you renovate it yourself?"

"Yep. It's all me," I said proudly.

"Great job."

"Thanks." I pointed at the open door. "Let me show you to your room. You're welcome to enjoy a nap while I tend to a few chores around the house."

Olivia yawned and nodded. "Great idea."

There were two bedrooms and a full bathroom downstairs that I used. The upstairs area, comprising three bedrooms and two bathrooms, remained permanently locked. I rarely went up there unless I wanted linen or something that I kept in the passage storage.

I showed Olivia to the smaller of the two rooms. The closet was empty, so if she wanted to go snooping, there would be nothing for her to rummage through.

As Olivia closed the door, she stopped and called me. "Thank you again for everything. One question," she asked, raising her index finger, and wincing slightly. "Can I ask how much you're paying me for a week's worth of cleaning?"

"I can afford fifty dollars."

Her eyes widened.

"That okay with you?"

She nodded profusely. "Yes, absolutely." Her smile reached her glistening eyes, and I was glad she closed the door before she burst into tears. I hated tears. The last thing I needed now was a happy woman crying.

Over the next three days, Olivia only cleaned the downstairs area. She swept, mopped, dusted, ensured the washing was done and even prepared all the meals. No job was too big or too small for her to do. She used my ladder to dust cobwebs from high corners, cleaned parts of the house that hadn't seen a cloth in decades, and she did it all without complaining.

As much as I enjoyed having her around, I would much prefer having her in her own room downstairs with the rest of my *Keys*. She was pretty to watch; she wore those small shorts that showed everything, and she never wore a bra. She was someone to talk with, but she invaded my personal space more than I liked.

The itch at the back of my neck intensified by the end of the third day. I didn't want her around me anymore. The house smelled of spring fresh. Things were clean and different; nothing was where I had left it. And it wasn't the way I cleaned. I hated it.

While she was mopping the veranda, I went to my basement to prepare her new room; her forever home.

She'd be here by nightfall.

I didn't wait until nightfall.

Olivia had just finished showering and entered her room when I came in behind her and started choking her. She surprised me by unlatching herself from my grip, but before she could get away, I slammed my fist into her face. She doubled over, blood pouring out of her nose, and I caught her before she fell to the ground, unconscious.

I lifted her over my shoulder and carried her to the kitchen and down the basement stairs, and just as I got halfway, she woke up and started fighting me.

Angry, I turned on the stairs, raised her legs, and lifted her off my shoulders. She flew off behind me, her head hitting the stairs. Blood sprayed everywhere, and I swore under my breath; it would take forever to clean up that mess. But I forgave her as I watched with excitement how she fell down the stairs like a rag doll. When she reached the bottom; she was finally quiet.

"You don't learn, do you, Olivia?" I said, jogging down the stairs, ensuring I didn't step in the blood, and stood over her body.

She continued moaning incoherently. Her nose had broken further, there was a gash on one side of her head, and her left eye had already begun swelling. She had broken her right elbow and scraped her knees. She needed urgent medical attention, and I grabbed the first aid kit as I dragged her by her foot across the basement floor and down the two steps through the metal lockers and into my beautiful domain.

I pulled her into her new room and onto her mattress. I crouched near her face and arm and started cleaning wounds with antiseptic ointment. Her nose would forever be skew as it healed, so there was nothing I could do about that. I stitched everything else with those butterfly strips and plaster.

Once I was done, I injected her with an anti-inflammatory and painkiller I made from my potent garden; it wouldn't kill her, just keep her relaxed and helped her to heal. The last thing I wanted was my poor number 5 to suffer. I was not cruel and loved all my *Keys*. I hoped to get more of these beauties so that I could fill every space down here.

I picked up the trash and first aid kit and locked the door behind me while she rested. There were things I needed to discuss with her; rules I needed to explain. Rules were very important to me, and I needed to ensure she would obey every single one of them.

I sat on the porch swing chair and sipped on my iced tea while looking up at the moon and stars. *Key* number 5 should wake soon, and I wanted to be there when she did; at least it was a friendly face she would wake up to.

With my free hand, I held my keychain and rubbed *Key* number 5 between my thumb and index finger. This was her new home, here with me; nothing and nobody would take her away from me.

The wind blew, and I shivered. I finished my iced tea and stood up. It was time.

"Olivia," I sang, pushing loose strands of hair out of her face. "Wakey-wakey."

Olivia stirred and moaned at the same time. I placed the pouch on the ground and helped her to sit up. She stared at me through one eye. The other now swollen shut. She coughed and winced.

"I'm glad you're still alive and looking so well." I lied, of course, and crouched near her again. She looked terrible.

All I needed now was for her to cry again and her look would be complete. It was a pity her face was so swollen and bruised, it ruined her natural beauty.

"There are rules you need to follow, Key Number Five." She stared deadpan at me. "Nod if you understand." She nodded. "Good. Rule number one is never call out. There are others here, and they understand the rules. They follow the rules because they know if they step out of line, they will be in big trouble. Nod if you understand me." She pursed her lips, glancing away, but nodded.

I stood up and towered over her. "Look at me," I commanded in a deep and throaty voice. My *Key* obeyed, craning her neck to look at me. "Good, rule number two is never fight me." She blinked. "And the last rule is whenever I enter your little room, you do everything I want. Okay?" She pursed her lips even more and blinked. She glanced away, and a tear slipped down her cheek.

I grabbed the pouch from the floor and searched for the item I needed.

Olivia moved and winced as her broken elbow twisted. That caused me pain just watching her.

"Let me ease the discomfort for you," I said, stepping closer.

"Stay away from me," she hissed, scooting backward. She bumped her head against the wall behind her, not taking her eyes off me.

I stood straight and scowled. "You're already breaking the rules, Olivia."

"Please, Jack," she said, crying. "Please let me go. I promise I won't say anything. Just let me go and I'll forget all about you."

"Now, why would I want to do that? You're my new favorite *Key*, Olivia. I want you to remember me for the rest of your life. I wouldn't give you up for all the gold in the world." Leaning closer, I added, "You're very special to me." She turned her face away from me, and I planted a delicate kiss on her cheek. "See, no pain there."

She wiped her face where I'd just kissed her with her hand.

I removed the cap from the sharp needle.

"What's that?" she asked nervously.

"Just something to help with your pain." I cleaned the area and inserted the needle into her arm. My motions were slow and calculated; I wanted her to feel the too large needle slicing the skin and digging into her arm. Then I wanted her to feel the cool liquid enter her system as it travelled from her arm down to her hand and spread across her chest, abdomen, hips and lastly down to her legs, feet, and toes.

I slowly pulled the needle out of her skin, wiped blood away, and helped her get comfortable on the mattress.

Her eyes flittered closed.

Her mouth fell open.

And her arms fell limply at her sides.

Leaning over, I kissed both cheeks and gently touched her face. "See, all better now."

I covered the needle with the plastic cap and placed it inside the pouch. Picking up the lantern, I closed the door behind me and locked it. I pressed my palm against the door near the number "5" and kissed the brass.

"Welcome home."

Chapter Twenty

MICHELLE GONE MISSING

Detective Steve Campbell
2002

I used the bathroom and found Alice sitting in her chair, staring out at the mountains behind our house.

We were lucky to find this double story house in Ketchum. Ever since the residential boom where celebrities and multimillion-dollar mansion owners from Sun Valley and Ketchum had forced lower-, middle- and some upper-income families out, making it difficult to find an affordable home.

The previous owner of this house had slipped, cracked her head, and bled in the bathroom, tainting the house. Her children wanted to rid themselves of this property soonest, therefore, making it affordable for us to buy on my detective's salary; the generous increase offered by the Ketchum Police Department helped.

"I'm on my way," I said, leaning on my good knee and kissing her left cheek.

She turned her head and glanced up, offering me a weak smile. "Have a good day at work. I hope the phone call wasn't anything too serious? You said you would take today off," she said with sadness in her tone.

"I know," I said, reaching for her hand and squeezing gently. I hated leaving her home alone again. "It's a missing girl, and I should be home after lunch. Then we can pack the picnic basket and go to the lake. How does that sound?" I asked.

"Sounds good," she said meekly, turning to look out of the window again.

"Will you walk outside for me today?" I asked. Alice hadn't left the house since we moved from Las Vegas to Ketchum about a month ago.

"Uh-huh," she said absentmindedly, still staring out of the window.

I stared at her as my heart broke. Alice used to be outgoing and vibrant, now she was a shadow of her former self. I missed the woman I married, but I had to be patient. She had two miscarriages last year, and the doctor advised not to try again for a few months. She hadn't wanted me to touch her since the last time she was in hospital almost four months ago. And moving here also took its toll on her.

I loved Alice. She had been the woman for me since high school and I would take the rest of my life to ensure she lived as comfortable as possible, giving her all the time she needed to heal.

I leaned down and kissed her cheek again. She didn't budge. I wouldn't take it personally. She was still grieving for the baby boy and girl we would never meet. She had lost both babies in the third trimester; which was traumatic for her. There was something wrong, and no doctor understood what it was. Nobody had an answer that could explain to us what we needed to do for her to carry a baby to full term.

I entered the station and found him sitting in a visitor's chair. "Mike," I said, proffering a hand. "It's good to see you again."

Mike stood up, combing his fingers through his shaved hair. "Hi, yes, sorry I heard it was your day off, but there wasn't anyone else who could help, and you know about Jessica's disappearance."

"Don't worry about it. Now tell me what happened."

For the next hour, Mike told what had happened to Michelle. First it was her friend, Jessica, and now her. It was too coincidental that the two friends had both gone missing from the same pub only a couple of weeks apart. And I couldn't ignore the fact that it could be the same kidnapper.

I first met Mike and Michelle when I worked on Jessica's case. They were distraught when she disappeared. There was not much I could do because there were no witnesses, no evidence... nothing. Unfortunately, I had to abandon her case for a double homicide. Now I wished I had tried harder, but there was nothing to point us in any direction.

I hoped it would be different now.

Since the other detectives were out at various scenes, I thanked Mike for coming to me directly and I called a junior police officer to accompany me to O'Brian's Pub. I needed to ensure we covered everything and spoke to all who might have seen Michelle last night.

We arrived soon after they had opened. Nancy was tending to the bar while Pat was in his office.

"Detective," Nancy said while wiping down the bar. "Are you here for a meal or a drink?"

"Official business, I'm afraid."

"Oh?" she said and stopped wiping the counter. Her thick, dark brows knitted together as concern flashed in her features. She had tied her peroxided blond hair in a low ponytail, her lips were bright red, and she wore the standard black t-shirt and jeans. She reminded me of a character in the program, Sons of Anarchy.

"Do you remember seeing either of these two women?" I held up the photos Mike had given me. The original photo I had of Jessica had torn, and I was grateful for a new and clearer picture of her face. "If you'll recall, I was here about this one who went missing about three weeks ago," I showed her the picture of Jessica, "and this one went missing last night." I raised the picture of Michelle.

Nancy furrowed her brows and took the photos from my hands. "Like I said then, I don't remember Jessica." She waved Michelle's photo. "Yeah, I remember this one. She came in asking for someone to help jump start her car, and Jack helped her."

"Jack who?"

"Haskins," she said. Her eyes flitted from mine to Officer Graham, who stood behind me. "You don't think Jack has anything to do with this?" she asked with concern in her tone.

"I don't know," I said honestly, "but I'd like to know who this Jack Haskins is."

"His great grandfather and family started farming here years ago and helped the town grow," Nancy said matter-of-factly. "And if I'm not mistaken, and if one excluded celebrities, they're one of the richest families here. I've known Jack all my life, and he's never been involved in anything like this before."

Officer Graham shook his head. "We don't know that he's connected, Nancy," he said. "We'll investigate and follow the trail wherever it may lead."

"Good, because he really is a nice guy. He comes in here every Saturday for a steak or burger, and we always have pleasant conversation. I've never seen or heard him do anything untoward."

"Can we chat with Pat quickly?" I thumbed toward his office.

"Yeah, sure," she said, pointing at the open office door.

I nodded my thanks, heading that way, and knocked on the door frame. Pat turned slowly in his swivel chair, smiling. "The new detective finally gracing us with his presence. What can I do for you?"

I asked him the same question I'd asked Nancy, but he wasn't here last night and couldn't help us.

"And you still don't have any cameras?" I'd asked Nancy this question when I was investigating Jessica's disappearance because Pat had been away that week and I didn't need to speak with him at all.

"Goodness no," Pat said, shaking his head. "If I did that, I'd lose most of my customers. You know what it's like."

Unfortunately, I did. I'd seen what happened in a small town. People met at bars, drank too much, and ended up going home with someone else's husband or wife. People didn't want to frequent an establishment when someone could use evidence against them during a divorce.

Officer Graham's radio sounded. There was a vehicle matching Michelle's discovered at the Old Mill.

"Thanks Pat," I said, heading for the exit.

"Let us know if you need anything else, detective," Pat said as we were leaving. "And come by for a free meal, you and your beautiful wife."

"Thanks, and we will." I waved goodbye.

Alice and I had been here for about a month and was yet to see everything this town offered or hid. Everyone already knew who I was, which meant news travelled quick here.

I had met almost everyone in the police station and had avoided conversations where other people were discussed; I hated gossip.

"What's this place?" I asked Officer Graham. I hadn't explored this side of Ketchum yet, so it intrigued me to know more.

"The Old Mill closed their doors about five years ago," he said seriously. "They employed the homeless to make wooden furniture."

"Do you know why they closed?"

"The owner was using it to sell drugs." Officer Graham sounded exhausted or sad, or a combination of the two. The station was understaffed, therefore everyone worked overtime and was exhausted. They hoped by bringing me in, I could assist with the caseload.

I parked my car behind the lab technician's car and watched Officer Graham with interest. His uniform was neat, his dark red hair shaved close to his head, and when he smiled it brightened his green eyes; but he didn't smile often. He was in his early thirties, and I was curious why he hadn't moved up the ranks yet.

"Is there anything else you can tell me about the place?" I asked, not wanting to exit the car just yet.

Officer Graham turned to face me. "You're new here," he said in a serious tone, "so let me rather tell you my version before you hear something from someone twisting the truth." He sighed, glancing at the Old Mill, then back at me.

"My father started this furniture business, and it flourished. But then," he paused for a moment and blinked slowly, "one of his old friends introduced him to bad people. They wanted my father to sell their product using his wooden furniture to get through customs, but then my dad started using the product without paying for it. By then I had just started my fourth year on the force and the Sheriff wanted to promote me to detective. Nobody had moved within the ranks so quickly. Then everything came crashing down." He jerked his chin toward the Old Mill.

"That must've been hard," I offered as I imagined the humiliation, frustration, and disappointment he must've endured. "Where's your dad now?"

"He killed himself." Officer Graham reached for the door handle and climbed out.

I gave him a moment alone and counted to ten, then I opened my car door and joined him. I didn't know what else to say, so thought it best not to say anything at this moment.

We headed for the group of men surrounding the midnight blue 1997 Ford Crown Victoria that had its doors, hood, and trunk open.

Officer Graham followed closely behind me and tipped his head in greeting. The men ignored him and said 'hi' to me. I felt sorry for Officer Graham but also admired him; they ostracized him, yet he continued to serve and protect. I doubted many could do that.

"What do we have here?" I asked.

"Steve," James, the lab technician, said. He nodded at Officer Graham, pulled on a fresh pair of gloves, and handed me a pair. "Come, look here. I waited for your arrival before bagging the evidence I found in the trunk."

We walked around the car and he pointed at the bloody rag, black t-shirt, and a knife. "I'll let you know the moment we have any fingerprints and results from the DNA samples I collected."

"Mike had said Jessica wore a black t-shirt with The Rolling Stones tongue on the front. Can you open the shirt for me?"

James did as I asked and showed me the t-shirt. "I thought Michelle went missing," he said.

"Yeah, but her friend Jessica disappeared early December."

James whistled. "Hectic. I don't remember Jessica's case." James bagged the items and took a few more samples.

"We didn't have any evidence for you to collect when she disappeared, but what concerns me is why is her t-shirt inside of Michelle's vehicle. Which means their disappearances are connected."

"Maybe it's their friend," Officer Crick said. When we arrived, he had greeted me and avoided all eye contact with Officer Graham. At least James greeted Officer Graham in some way. But this wasn't my problem, unfortunately Officer Graham still had a long road ahead of him. My problem was solving this case, but I'd keep an eye on Officer Crick. There was something about him I didn't like and needed more time before offering an opinion.

"Already checked Mike out, and it's not him," I said. The silence stretched between us as we watched James carefully remove all the evidence and swab stains and anything wet or red. "Can you tell me more about Jack Haskins?"

Officer Crick's eyebrows arched. "Jack? Why him?"

"Nancy said he helped Michelle out last night," I said. "They left together, but neither returned."

"Jack is harmless," Officer Crick said, with James nodding and mumbling his agreement. "He's odd, but he mostly keeps to himself. He's friendly when he's in town on Saturdays and everybody knows him."

"Thanks," I said. What I didn't say was I would still investigate him. Everybody was a suspect until proven otherwise. "I'm just going to look around." I pointed at the abandoned building.

Officer Crick and James waved goodbye and continued their private conversation while Officer Graham followed behind me.

"What are you looking for?" he asked.

"I don't know," I said absentmindedly. I walked along the broken fence bordering the Old Mill. My boots sunk into deep snow as I traversed along the border and was careful not to hurt my right knee after a car accident I'd been in, in my twenties.

The Old Mill was on a slight hill that overlooked the town; the view was scenic and almost pleasant if it weren't for the broken car filled with blood and evidence.

As I neared the Old Mill building, the smell of urine assaulted my nose, along with something burning inside; most likely cardboard to keep the homeless warm. Officer Graham walked beside me now and covered his nose with his hand.

"Not sure I want to go in there," he said, standing still.

"Yeah, me neither," I said, pointing to one side. We walked in silence as we rounded the corner and headed toward the back part of the Old Mill that overlooked the mountains. "It's beautiful here," I said. "Does this piece of land still belong to your family?"

"Nah, the bank took it back after all the mess and couldn't secure a buyer. We approached Jack to see if he wouldn't buy it, but he declined. He had said he had nothing he could do with it." He stopped and glanced around with sadness in his eyes.

"I'm just going to check inside the vehicle quickly and then we can head back to the station."

"Sure," Officer Graham said, heading in my vehicle's direction.

I peered inside Michelle's car on the driver's side, noting the seat was more forward, perfect for a female or a short male.

I grabbed another pair of gloves, slipped them on, and looked inside the glove compartment; but there was nothing of interest. There was nothing under the seat or carpet. The backseat had a few empty wrappers but nothing of significance. I would have to wait for the results after James had them processed.

"I want to check and see if there are any cases similar to our current missing females," I said to Officer Graham as we climbed into my car and closed our doors.

Officer Graham nodded. "I can do that for you. Is there anything specific I should search for?"

I pulled out onto the road, turned around, and headed back to the station. "I'm going to drop you off at the station and I'll go to her mom's place. Mike had said she lives somewhere in Sun Valley." We headed down the road and I applied brakes. I'd been going a little too fast and didn't want Officer Graham thinking I disobeyed the rules.

I was silent for a moment, thinking about what he could search for, and concentrated on the road, then when I stopped outside the station, I kept the car idling. "Search for any women between the ages of eighteen and twenty-four who went missing near Ketchum, Sun Valley, or were passing through. I know it may be a little tricky but see what you can find."

Officer Graham nodded and climbed out, tipping his head in greeting.

Now to see if there was anything at Michelle's mom's place that could help me.

Chapter Twenty-One

MORE GIRLS GONE

Detective Steve Campbell
2002

Michelle's mom's place was near the mobile home park near Clear Creek and Big Wood River. It was one of the smaller homes with only one bedroom and I assumed Michelle slept on the couch in the lounge. I knocked on the door, but nobody answered.

"Ain't nobody home," a man said, sticking his head out of the window of his mobile home across the street. "Ain't anybody home usually."

"Where's the mom?"

"Michelle's adoptive mom hasn't been home since she left with that businessman a couple of months ago, and Michelle is working hard at the one resort."

I approached the man's mobile home and handed him one of my cards. "If you see anyone enter this place or come looking for either mom or daughter, can you call me?"

"Yep, will do," the man said, taking my card. "The name is Lukas." He smiled.

"Thanks, Lukas. I'm Detective Steve Campbell." I headed back to my car, waved at him when he waved, and drove back to the station.

The trip to Michelle's home was a waste of time, but at least now I knew where her mother was, and why she hadn't come in saying Michelle was missing. I would contact her though to let her know what was happening.

I arrived back at the station, but before I could go to my office, Officer Graham called me over with excitement.

"Please tell me you've found something?" I said with a sigh and sat in a chair near his desk.

Officer Graham grinned. "Sure have." He tapped on his keyboard. "Many people travel through Ketchum when either going to Boise or Salt Lake City. They would go to Twin Falls and then come our way for the touristy things and maybe find work, so I searched for any female who went missing while traveling this way."

"That makes sense," I said, my interest piqued. "And casting a wider net may include way too many, so keeping it closer makes sense. If we need to go wider, include missing women from Montana and Washington."

"Precisely," Officer Graham said with a nod. "I went back ten, twenty years and I found six women in our database who had disappeared near here. All the relatives had said the women went specifically through Ketchum."

"Six women," I said, shaking my head. "Who are they?"

"Excluding our current missing women, there's Kate. She was twenty-one-years-old and missing since 1987. She and her partner were at her mom's cabin for the weekend. Her partner went into anaphylactic shock after an allergic reaction. Kate's mom phoned the police when she didn't come home and they found drops of Kate's blood near the man's body. Next, we have Brook, nineteen, and Marley, seventeen, who were on holiday together when they went missing in 1989."

I shook my head. The eighties and nineties were not safer than they were now, and to think young girls travelled together was beyond me. I also understood that life circumstances forced some children to grow up quicker than others and, although they were street smart, bad things still happened to nice kids.

"In 1991, nineteen-year-old Olivia went missing. Some folks saw her walking around town asking for work. In 1993 seventeen-year-old Stacey was waiting for the bus, and in 1995 nineteen-year-old Susan went outside to smoke a cigarette and didn't return."

Officer Graham handed the original case files to me.

"Thanks," I said, glancing at the six files in my hands. "If this is the same guy, there must be more. It's as if he finds a woman every year."

Officer Graham nodded, pushing his chair closer to his table, and started tapping away on his keyboard again. "I'm going to widen the search to other states."

I nodded while glancing at the cases. "He likes them young—"

"Naïve," Officer Graham interjected. "He likes them innocent and unsure of themselves, even though they're traveling alone or with a friend."

"How old do you think this guy is?"

"Probably your age," he said, grinning.

"What? Old?" I chuckled.

"Early forties?" he asked.

"Yep," I said. "But he could also be late thirties, and definitely a white male."

"Yep," Officer Graham said, "and he knows this town." His computer pinged with another list of results. "Missy, eighteen in 1990. Leanna, eighteen, 1992. Maggie, eighteen, also 1993. Nancy, eighteen in 1995. Janice, seventeen, 1997. And Brandy, nineteen, 1999. I'll put in a request for the original case files to be brought to us."

"Thanks," I said. "So some years he has two girls."

"They could've been friends," he added.

"Or the opportunity presented itself."

Officer Graham nodded. "It makes me sick," he said with disgust. "I hate this."

"We'll find the bastard," I said confidently. "He'll make a mistake." I shifted in my seat when three cases fell to the floor, spilling pages. I reached down and picked them up when my eye caught a name. "Jacob Haskins?" I said. "Does Jack Haskins have a brother?"

"No," Officer Graham said, frowning, and glanced at the piece of paper I was reading. "Which case is that?"

"Kate," I said, reading the top. "Kate Mary Pryce. It says here she was a friend of Jacob Haskins." I raised the sheet and pointed.

Officer Graham frowned, turned to his keyboard, and typed some more. "Jacob changed his name to Jack, so it's the same person." He was silent as he read from the screen and mumbled words I couldn't hear. "He had been looking for Kate the day she disappeared, but he wasn't a suspect because his parents said he was home all evening."

"He could've left while they were sleeping."

"Yep." Officer Graham sat back and folded his arms across his chest, his jaw ticking. "I'm younger than him and lived here my whole life, and I've never heard a bad thing about the man. But it's more than just a coincidence we have two cases where we mention his name."

"I agree," I said. "Luckily, I don't know him at all and can look at it from a fresh perspective. But I need to know more about him."

"You can start with his parents," Officer Graham said, tapping away at the keyboard. "I'll bring the original case file to you once I get them."

I stared wide eyed at him. "They're dead?"

"Yeah," Officer Graham said. "Home invasion gone wrong and only a couple of months after Kate went missing."

"Now I'm very suspicious of the guy," I said with a heavy sigh. "At least here it says they also hurt him," I said, pointing at the computer screen where the detective in charge described how Jacob had a knife lodged in his back when he ran away from the intruder. Jacob also sustained an injury to his head.

"They had taken their jewelry and, according to Jacob, his parents had nothing else worth stealing and they didn't know about the safe. Come to think of it," Officer Graham said, glancing at the screen, "nobody knew where the safe was and Jacob didn't elaborate either. It makes me wonder what's in the safe."

"Is he really still one of the richest family in town?" I asked.

"Nobody knows for sure, but yes, I think so. His piece of land stretches around the mountains at the entrance into Ketchum. He's had cattle, sheep, and even pigs. Now he grows sunflowers between April and mid-June and sells them to florists or manufacturers of sunflower oil."

"I did not know that, and do the flowers grow in snow?" I asked, my frown deepening.

"No, they generally die when snow first falls, but Jack has a personal garden which he grows in a large greenhouse which protects them from the elements. The result is he has sunflowers to look at all year round, and if I'm not mistaken, he still has a few if you want to look."

"I want to pay him a visit."

"I'd be careful though, or he'll have lawyers on you in no time. When Sheriff Adams was still alive, he tried to gain access to his property and before he could park his car, Jack's lawyers gave orders for the sheriff to move his car."

"Seriously?"

"Yep," Officer Graham sipped from his cold coffee. "I think Sheriff Adams wanted Jack to provide DNA samples voluntarily in a sexual assault case." He almost dropped the cup in his hand and frantically typed on his keyboard. "I can't believe I forgot about that," he said. "I'd just started on the force when a woman accused Jack of raping her. Sheriff Adams wanted DNA, but the girl dropped the case—"

"Probably paid her off."

"Yep."

"I'm starting not to like this guy." I folded my arms across my chest and leaned back.

"The girl passed away last year. It says here she had cancer."

"How convenient," I grumbled.

Chapter Twenty-Two

KATE'S MOM

Detective Steve Campbell
2002

The parents of the other missing women lived in different states, so I couldn't interview any of them face-to-face. But there was one mother who lived in Ketchum, and I knocked on her front door since there was no doorbell.

Someone opened the door wide enough for me to see their mature eyes. "Yes?" she croaked.

"Mrs. Pryce? I'm Detective Steve Campbell," I said, raising my badge high enough for her to see.

She opened the door wider and unlatched the hook for the screen door. "What's this about, detective?"

"I'm working a missing person's case and I believe it's connected to your missing daughter."

Mrs. Pryce paled slightly and clutched her chest.

"Are you okay?" I asked, readying to open the screen door and rush her to the hospital.

"I'm fine. You just caught me off guard." She pushed the screen door open and disappeared inside her house. "I'll put the kettle on."

I entered her house and closed the screen door behind me, latching it in place. Her living room was to my right and her open planned kitchen on the left. The kettle whistled and the clinking of cups as she worked quickly around her kitchen and as I reached her; she had already poured water into the cups.

"Let's sit over there," she said, pointing at the couches. "I haven't spoken about Katie in so long, but before we get there you mentioned a missing person."

I sat across from her and pulled out the two pictures. "This is Jessica, and this is Michelle. They're best friends and were kidnapped about a month apart, and we believe by the same person."

"Oh, dear me," she said, reaching for the photos and squinting at them. She reached for the glasses hanging around her neck and slipped them on for a better look. "Poor girls." She shook her head, and handed them back to me. She leaned back and had a drink of tea.

I waited a moment before peppering her with questions. I sipped the tea, and it had the right amount of tea versus honey ratio.

She set her teacup on the table between us and sat back. "Right. What would you like to know?"

"What can you tell me about your daughter's disappearance?"

She shook her head. "Katie started dating this businessman. Now what was his name?" she said, thinking, and waving an imaginary fly away. "Can't remember. Anyway, they went to my cabin for the weekend and neither of them returned. Her blood was everywhere, and that poor man had cayenne pepper in his food. He was deadly allergic to it, mind you. Poor man."

It was what I had already read in the police file. "Do you have an idea who took your daughter?" There was no mention of anyone interviewing her in the file and I wondered whether the man she was seeing, Sheriff Adams, did that on purpose to protect her.

She pursed her lips and closed her eyes. When she opened her eyes again, hate filled her features. "I never like that boy. I always told Katie there was something wrong with him. But she said he was nice to her." She shook her head. "I should've been stricter on her, but who was I to say who she could be friends with."

"Who is this?"

"That Jacob Haskins boy. He goes by the name of Jack now. He's a very troubled man. I heard rumors about his family, all hearsay, mind you."

"What rumors?"

"Just that his family on his mom's side was trouble; lowlives and convicts. That's why none of them ever visited. Anyway, when Sheriff Adams questioned the boy, his parents said he was home all evening, and he couldn't continue with the investigation because there was nothing else to go on."

"Did you hear any rumors about other women going missing?"

"Plenty," she said, picking up her teacup and sipping. "He raped that poor girl who died of cancer. My friend Betty found the poor girl crying. Her clothing had been torn, blood between her legs. It was just awful."

"Where is Betty now so that I can speak with her?"

"Oh goodness, Betty's long gone, detective."

I sighed inwardly. Although I couldn't question Betty, at

least I was getting a good idea about Jack. "Some people have said that Jack is a nice man. That he doesn't bother anyone, and he's always friendly."

She sneered. "They don't really know him. Jack has many poisonous layers to his personality, and I would be afraid to find out what his center looks like. Most probably dripping in dark horrors." She shuddered.

"Do you know if Sheriff Adams ever searched Jack's farmhouse?"

"He didn't allow him. Bill, Jack's stepfather, blatantly refused. Told the sheriff to come with a warrant. Obviously, Sheriff Adams never did, there wasn't enough reason to." She fell silent for a moment and stared at her hands. When she wiped a tear away, I knew I'd reached the end of our conversation. She'd been through enough, and I didn't want to hurt her more than she already was. But before I left I had to ask one more question.

"Is there anything else you can think of?"

Mrs. Pryce finished her tea, closed her eyes, leaned back into her chair and sighed. I was about to stand when she sat up. "I can't remember the boys name but soon after we moved here and Katie became friends with Jacob or Jack or whatever his name is. This boy disappeared. Katie told me he used to bully Jacob, then one day, gone." She sighed wearily.

"And my Toby, otherwise known as Sheriff Adams. He was having lunch at the diner when Jack came in and spoke with him. Now I can't prove anything but one moment Jack is there, he leaves, and my Toby convulses and dies. His face in his soup. The doctors said it was a heart attack so who am I to argue, but it didn't sit right with me, you know. I know in my heart it was that boy."

"I'll look into both and see what I can come up with."

"Good, I hope you find something." She wiped another tear and it was time I left. I had more than enough information with more to look up, but it was a good start.

I finished the rest of my tea and stood up. "Thank you for answering my questions and for the tea." I raised my cup.

"Pleasure," she said, picking up her teacup and followed me to the kitchen.

I set my teacup in the sink.

"I hope you get everything you need to put him away. And I know my Katie is gone," she glanced at a photo on the wall near her fridge, "I hope you can find these two girls so they can return to their parents." She smiled thinly and headed for the front door.

"Thanks again," I said, handing her a business card. "If you think of anything else, please call me."

I left Mrs. Pryce and headed for my car, and I knew we were on the right path.

I returned to the station and informed Officer Graham about my visit, along with the additional information about Sheriff Adams and the young boy.

After thirty minutes Officer Graham called me over.

"Dylan Edwards was eleven-years-old when he disappeared. His friends were the last to see him. They were on their bikes and went their separate ways to their homes, but Dylan didn't reach his destination."

"And nobody saw where he went?" I asked, eating a chicken and mayo sandwich.

"No," Officer Graham said, clicking the mouse. "And Sheriff Adams died of natural causes." He shrugged.

"So there's nothing?"

"I'm afraid so."

I watched another officer enter and sit behind his desk. He had a plaster on his arm from having bloods taken. "Was a toxicology report done for Sheriff Adams?"

Officer Graham shook his head.

"Any bloods or samples. Not sure if any traces can still be found. I don't know, I'm thinking out loud."

"I can find out."

"Please do."

Chapter Twenty-Three

PACE ITCH THINK KEYS

Jack
2002

I paced in the living room toward the fireplace, down the hallway, touched the wall and then paced back to the living room mantlepiece.

The itch at the back of my neck only intensified, and the more I scratched, the more it burned.

As I paced, the itch seemed to move up and down the length of my spine and then spread to my shoulders. The fresh wound in the middle of my neck ached, and I rubbed it instead of scratching.

With one hand I rubbed the back of my neck, while the other held the keychain holding my precious *Keys*. So many delicious *Keys* who kept me company. They were the reason I got out of bed in the mornings. They were my everything. My life was finally worth living since accumulating them.

I remembered my first *Key* like it happened yesterday. Oh, Katie was the best, the one who started it all; she awoke something within me.

Something so strong and wild; primal.

I still remembered her smell, as if she was right here beside me now. Her smell had changed over time, and she now greeted me with a smile whenever I entered her room. She understood I was there to protect her and ensure she ate, washed herself, and exercised. Her living quarters were small, like the others, and they all managed just fine. They were all happy being down there with me.

But, after that woman escaped, I knew the day would arrive when someone knocked on my door needing more information about a missing woman.

The new detective was on the case and as much as I hated him, I had to listen to what he had to say. He had called earlier asking to meet with me—and permission to enter my land—and as much as I wanted to say no; I wanted to find out what he knew.

I continued pacing toward the mantlepiece and placed the keychain on the hook, walked to the other side and back again. I picked up the keychain and paced once more. Up and down. Scratching the back of my neck. Thinking.

I switched on the lights in the bathroom, washed my face, dried the water off with a towel, flicked the light off, and continued pacing.

Since I no longer used upstairs, I only switched on the lights in my bedroom and the spare bedroom. Then I switched them off again. Up and down. Scratching. Thinking. Flicking light switches on and off. Placing the keychain on the mantlepiece, paced up and down the hallway, fetched it again. Up and down. Scratching. Thinking. Over and over.

My stomach grumbled. My feet ached. And exhaustion washed over me. I'd lost track of time, and four hours had passed. Pocketing my keychain, I entered the kitchen. I'd made bangers and mash hours ago and the meal waited for me in the oven. I took it out, sat at the table and ate the cold food.

Mama always made her food too hot, with too much salt, and too much butter. The food I made was always flavorful, with only a dash of salt and butter. I also watched what I ate, ensuring my body was fit and my mind alert.

I sipped my milk and finished the last of the food. For a few moments, I sat at the table, steepled my fingers, and stared out of the window. The wind blew through the trees nearby, making them look like they're waving at me.

I moved my head to the left, then right, and once my neck clicked and released, did I relax. The tension that had been building between my shoulder blades seemed to aggravate my neck muscles.

I stood up from the antique wooden table. My fingers finding the spot I had desecrated when I was seven and smiled. I had felt good that day; Mama had screamed at me because I'd scraped some pieces of wood off the corner. The table was an antique. It first belonged to my great grandfather, and everybody had used it through the years.

I rubbed the dented wood and smiled at the fond memory, but sadness overwhelmed me at the thought that I would never have a child of my own who would sit at the table, and I didn't know how I felt about that. I'd never thought about having a child again after Katie; maybe I should think about it some more.

I picked up my plate, scraped the bits of food into the dustbin, and washed it in the sink along with my knife, fork, and glass. I placed the items in their place on the drying rack, moved the cloth neatly over the sink and paused, staring out at the tree waving at me. The same tree I used to climb and hide in until it was dinner time.

Snow wasn't falling tonight, and it wasn't as cold, but there was a chill in the house.

Then I looked at my beautiful sunflowers and smiled. They were also a constant reminder of the things I had accomplished in my life, always bringing me joy.

Turning around, I cocked my head to the side and frowned. The clock on the wall no longer ticked. I opened the drawer and took out new batteries and replaced the old ones. Once it started ticking again, I smiled. There, everything was perfect again.

Key number 1 called out to me as I squeezed the keychain in my hand. Rubbing the *Key* between my fingertips and warmth spread up my arm and into my chest. I wanted to go to her; I needed to go to her, but I couldn't. Not now.

"Soon, my lovely, then I'll be with you." I glanced at the clock, then at my wristwatch and the times matched. "Ten more minutes and the detective will be here," I mumbled to myself.

At 5:03 p.m., someone knocked on the door.

I only opened on the third knock.

"Jack Haskins?" the man said at my front door.

I eyed him narrowly. He stood a head taller than me, sandy blond hair, green eyes, broad shoulders, athletic build, and seemed the type who played football. The only reason he was a detective was because he destroyed his knee, and a family member was on the force; *possibly*. He stood firmly on both legs, but I noticed his right leg was bent slightly at the knee. He held up his badge. I squinted at his name; Detective Steve Campbell.

"Yes," I said with a nod.

"I'm Detective Campbell, I called earlier."

"I remember," I said, opening the screen door wider, "but you didn't say why you needed to speak with me."

The detective held out his hand for me to shake, but I stared at it. When he realized I would not entertain him, he pulled his hand back.

He coughed into his hand and continued, "It's regarding a missing Michelle Stanton." He held up a color photo of her. "We're asking everyone who was at O'Brian's Pub on Saturday. Nancy said you spoke with the missing woman and left with her."

"Oh yes, poor girl. I helped jump start her car and then I left her in the parking lot. She wanted to let her car idle for a bit before leaving."

The detective nodded and scribbled on his notepad. When he was done, he glanced up and to his right, at the wall on my left where the mirror used to hang. He blinked and glanced at me.

"Did you see anyone else in the area before you left her alone?"

I shook my head slowly as I thought about it. "No, but there was a group of men who exited while I was busy with her vehicle. Otherwise no, I recall no one else."

"Do you mind if I look around?"

"Do you have a warrant?" I asked, closing the door slightly so that he could no longer see the wall where the mirror used to be. I knew my rights, and I also knew that once I allowed him inside, he would poke around everywhere he didn't belong. The best thing for me was to be courteous without giving in to his requests unless he had legal documents. I also knew that offering him something to drink would help me, but I didn't feel like being that nice today.

"No," he said, raising his hands in mock surrender, "but I will get one if it's needed." He smiled.

The itch at the back of my neck started up again, and I pressed my sweaty palms against my pants. "I've done nothing wrong, detective, other than help a woman in need. And I know my rights."

"I understand," he said, making more notes on his pad. He knew his evidence was circumstantial and, unless he had physical proof, I had done something to this woman. He had nothing to stand on.

One important fact I learned was Michelle hadn't gone to the cops. If that were true, she would be standing beside him right now and he'd have a warrant, which he didn't.

"Do you go to the pub often?" he asked, shifting from side to side. His knee was probably aching, and he needed to move around.

"I'm there most Saturdays to enjoy a delicious meal and then I come home. Have you tried their steak and burger?"

"No, not yet."

"You've only been here a month, isn't that right?"

The detective arched an eyebrow and said, "That's right."

"It's a small town. I was at the post office when Kip and Gladys told me there was a fancy new detective in town." I smiled. "Welcome. I hope you enjoy living here."

"Thank you."

"You're originally from Las Vegas?"

"That's right."

"I can imagine what the crime must be like there. I'm sorry one of your first cases is a missing person."

"Two, actually," he said, pulling out another photo. "Have you seen this woman?"

I took the picture from him and stared at her; it was my beautiful Jessica; my latest addition. "No," I said, shaking my head, "I don't recognize her. Did she go missing on Saturday with Michelle?"

"No, she disappeared before Christmas last year."

"I hope our town is safe, detective. It's the tourist season. The last thing we need is a town rampant with missing persons." I shook my head in shame. "I hope you find these women, detective."

"Me, too, Mr. Haskins."

I had nothing else to say and the detective had no more questions so he left. I waited half an hour before heading downstairs.

"Hello, my darling," I said, entering Jessica's room. "How are you feeling?"

She sat up with tears in her eyes. Her hair was dirty, and I noted she hadn't washed herself in a couple of days.

"It's okay, you're okay," I said with kindness in my tone. I needed to be gentle with this one still. "I won't let anything bad happen to you, nor will I allow anyone to take you away." I reached for her still swollen jaw and caressed her cheek. "Here, let me clean you," I said, reaching for the water bucket. It was cold but refreshing; the air was thick and warm. "There we go." I washed her arm, then her shoulder and back. Then I washed the parts of her face that were not swollen. She was still in pain, and I didn't want to hurt her again.

Once all clean, I sat with her for a moment, kissed her

cheek, and stood up to leave. But she looked at me with those sad eyes and as much as she wanted to go home, I couldn't allow her. I couldn't set any of my *Keys* free no matter what.

They were mine.

Forever.

Chapter Twenty-Four

PINK SUNFLOWER

Detective Campbell
2002

I climbed back into the car and stared at the large plantation-looking farmhouse.

"What did he say?" Officer Graham asked.

"Obviously he denies it," I said grumpily, implying they wouldn't need us if killers and kidnappers told the truth. "And he's watching us." I jerked my chin in the house's direction. "It's like a knife down my back."

"And I told the lab to test the blood in Michelle and Jessica's case and the samples Sheriff Adams collected during Jack's parent's attack."

"There were still samples?" I asked, relieved there was something. Back then, some cases were just put one side without digging deeper.

"Yep," he said, smiling.

"Why couldn't they use the samples for the rape case?"

"They couldn't find it," Officer Graham said, shaking his head. "When I called down for the original case files they said the box for his parent's was gone. I had to go down there myself. Someone had hidden it; it was by chance I found it in another case."

I shook my head. "That explains why Sheriff Adams wanted a new sample but he got kicked off Jack's property."

"I've opened an investigation into who may have done this."

"Whoever it was will be found out." I hoped.

"I'm sure something will materialize. These types of things always get found out."

"I couldn't agree more," I said, turning the ignition. "Thanks, your help on this case has been invaluable."

Officer Graham smile brightened his face, and I couldn't help but smile with him. He and I worked well together and I would ask that we continued to work together.

I drove down the driveway, then went off the road and around the piece of land.

"Where are you going?" Officer Graham said, grabbing hold of the handrail on the door and dashboard. "You're going to ruin your car."

"It's just a little bumpy, and besides, I want to see the sunflowers." I grinned as we veered to the right and over a small hill. Then, in the distance, I saw the glass structure. I parked the car and opened my door. "Come, let's take a quick look."

Officer Graham joined me, and we traversed through the field and came to the back end of the glass greenhouse.

"Wow," I said. "It's like he has his own weather system in there." There were rows and rows of sunflowers. Some had just bloomed while others were busy dying. And in the

The Last Girl

center, I saw something pink. "Is that a pink sunflower?" I stood on my toes.

Officer Graham climbed onto the ledge and pressed his body against the glass to keep from falling off. "Yep, one pink sunflower in full bloom. It's quite spectacular if you ask me." He jumped off the ledge and dusted his hands. "I think we should go," he said cautiously. "I don't see any cameras, but I suspect Jack may have hidden them."

"Yeah, sure," I said, turning around. We headed back down to the car, but I kept glancing over my shoulder at the vast piece of land that Jack owned. The land seemed to go on forever with the mountains behind him. I saw the farmhouse and the barn in the background.

"I wonder," Officer Graham started, then stopped when he opened the door.

"What?"

Still deep in thought, Officer Graham turned to me and said, "You know how some super rich people buy second houses like most have done here in Ketchum, while others dig up the ground and install bomb shelters... I wonder if Jack has other properties we haven't considered yet. I saw nothing in the records, but maybe I'm not looking in the right place."

"We can find out," I said, smiling. Officer Graham may have had some trouble with his father, but he was a good cop. He was great at researching and came up with awesome ideas.

The radio crackled; reception needed me to get home. Alice was looking for me.

I dropped Officer Graham at the station and came straight home. Alice was sitting in the living room with no clothing on and the curtains were wide open.

"Alice, darling," I said, approaching carefully. "Are you okay, honey?" I glanced around and grabbed the sofa throw, draping it around her shoulders. "Alice?" I reached for her chin and gently moved her head so she could look me in the eye. "Babe, what are you doing on the floor?"

"Hi," she said, smiling, but the vacant look in her eyes told me she had one or two tablets she shouldn't have. All her meds seemed to numb her a bit too much and helped her do things she wouldn't otherwise do. "I was hungry and needed to sit on the carpet. You should sit beside me." She pulled on my arm.

I crouched in front of her, and sat down with my legs crossed beneath me so that I was comfortable. I reached for her hands and kept them in mine. When I smiled, she smiled too. "I would love to sit with you on the carpet."

We sat like that; me holding her hands while she stared outside, and it hurt watching the woman I loved break into a tiny million pieces, and I could do anything to stitch her back together again. As I sat with her, I realized she needed more help than I thought and would do everything I could to get her back on her feet.

I sighed wearily as my mind wandered and I glanced at the boxes against the wall that still needed unpacking. But it was the item in the vase on the table near the front door that made me flinch.

Alice cried out in pain when I yanked her hands as I stood up, bringing her with me. I glanced around to see if there was anyone around, but it was just us.

"Sorry, honey," I said, wrapping the blanket around her

shoulders again. "Alice?" I cupped her face with my hands. "Tell me, babe, when did the flower come?"

"Huh?" she said, her eyes flitting from me to the front door. "What flower?"

I took her hand gently in mine and walked us over to the table. "The pink sunflower," I said, pointing at the beautiful Helianthus. "Can you remember where you got this?"

"Oh that, it's so pretty," she said dreamily. "I found it in the backyard after breakfast," she reached for the pink petals, "It was on the floor near the glass sliding door."

"I'll be right back," I said, kissing her on her forehead and ran toward the back door. I opened the sliding door and bolted outside. There was nothing untoward that I could see. I observed that the side gate remained locked and there were no disturbances in the flowerbeds. The back yard was as it always was.

My heart thundered in my chest as my breathing steadied. I slowly walked back inside the house to find Alice on the floor, half asleep. I scooped her into my arms and climbed the stairs to our bedroom. Carefully, I placed her in bed and covered her.

I stared down at my wife, and I didn't know what I would do if anyone tried to hurt her. If anything were to happen, Jack would be the first person I would interview.

Chapter Twenty-Five

MAMA

Jack
2002

I grinned at the thought that Detective Steve Campbell would be home round about now and would discover that I'd left him and poor little Alice a pretty sunflower. It wasn't a common yellow sunflower but one of my pretty pinks. I hoped they appreciated its beauty.

It wasn't as if I did something wrong. All I did was leave the pretty pink where his ailing wife could find it. She had been very naked and completely out of it when she opened the sliding door.

The detective could be happy she wasn't my type, or I would've snatched her then and there. But I had no more space for any newcomers and the *Keys* I had were plenty enough.

I finished my iced tea, rinsed the glass, and placed it

neatly on the drying rack and pushed my body away from the counter.

I wanted to go downstairs to be with a different *Key*, but something caught my eye, and I went to the staircase, stopping near the first step, and glanced up at the dusty banister and cobwebs that seemed to grow daily between the wooden poles of the staircase.

Mama's voice called out to me, and I smiled with unshed tears. She hadn't called my name in so long I thought I would've forgotten what her voice sounded like… but I could never forget. Not my mama.

I climbed the stairs and headed for their bedroom. My hand hovered above their bedroom doorknob. I grabbed it, inserted the key unlocking it and turned, opening the door.

I waved dust particles out of my face and sneezed. Standing at the foot of their bed, I imagined what they used to look like when I was a kid coming into their bedroom to say good morning. The days when Papa was still kind to me.

The whispers were louder here. Whispers I rarely heard unless I entered their room. The whispers of memories I wished I forgot, along with the sadness they brought. It was worse here. That's one reason I didn't enjoy coming here, but today was different. Today Mama called me. Mama needed me for a change.

Each part of the house gave me a feeling. I felt lonely in the large kitchen when I ate there by myself. Anger when I was in the living room area. And misery upstairs in my old room; which I had hoped would provide me with the escape I desperately needed but never received. It was only when I ventured outside and did the things I wasn't supposed to do, did I find solace. The things I did when I was young turned me into the man I was today.

And then always sadness in their room.

Upstairs was where most of the things had happened, the stories I had heard from my grandfather, the yelling and taunting from my father, or the confessions from my mother. A confession that changed my life forever.

But they're gone now. They had been gone for a very long time and I was better off without them. My real father was not a nice man, while the dad I grew up with was worse, and my mother did little to shield me.

I coughed into my hand and rounded my shoulders. The room was full of dust, insects, and cobwebs. The items they had placed on their bedside tables the night they were murdered had remained there. I didn't want to disturb a thing.

The right-hand side table was my mother's; she had a porcelain lamp her mother had given her as a wedding present, a picture of them on their wedding day beside it, her reading glasses, and a packet of cigarettes and matches. And on top of the cigarettes was her scorpion broach.

I eyed the broach narrowly and approached that side and crouched. I'd forgotten about the photo album she had kept there, and I pulled it out, dusting it. Dust particles danced in front of my face as the light that squeezed through the curtains highlighted them. I sneezed again and opened the old item.

The first few pages were of my parents on their wedding day, a couple of family pictures, and then of me when I was a baby. There was only one photo; the day I was born. The last page was of a woman; a young, beautiful woman who resembled my mother, and a wave of emotions coursed through me.

And then there it was, a memory of her…

Chapter Twenty-Six

A MEMORY - MAMA'S CONFESSION

Jacob - 10 years old
1976

Mama awoke early and wore her favorite blue floral dress. It was sunny outside, and I wanted to play, but mama called me downstairs for breakfast.

"Morning, Mama," I said as I entered the kitchen.

"Tell your daddy he must come inside for breakfast," she yelled.

"Yes, Mama," I said. My shoulders dropping slightly but I would do what my mama asked and ran outside to the barn where Papa was working. I entered the barn slowly and found Papa bending over a fence he was putting together. "Papa?" I said, nervously twisting my shirt in my hands.

"What do you want, Jacob? Can you see I'm busy? Hmm, do those eyes of yours work?" Papa said without glancing my way.

"Sorry, Papa, but Mama said you must come in for breakfast." I stepped backward so that I could feel the warmth of the sun against my back.

Cursing under his breath, Papa stood straight and rubbed his back. He looked up and his eyes met mine. "And stop calling me Papa. I am not your goddam Papa!" he yelled.

I flinched and shivered as a coldness I'd never felt before seemed to spread from my legs up to my tummy, chest and into my shoulders, but my cheeks burned. Then I blinked back tears as I glanced at the house and saw Mama standing there with her hands on her hips. I turned back to look at Papa and he was angry. His face was red, while his eyes seemed to glow. My chin trembled.

Something crashed behind me, and I glanced over my shoulder again and Mama had fallen down the stairs. "Mama!" I yelled and ran to her. "Papa, come quickly. Mama is on the floor." I ran as fast as I could, knocking my knees to the ground when I reached her. "Mama?" I said, grabbing her hand with mine, not wanting to let her go. "Are you okay?" I asked, watching her eyelids flitter open.

"It's ok, Jacob," Mama said, patting my hand as she slowly sat up. She glanced at Papa, who remained by the barn door, watching us as he cleaned his hands with a red cloth. "I'm fine," she said, turning to me with a thin smile. "It was just a dizzy spell. Come, let's have some breakfast."

I stood up and helped Mama stand. I didn't want to let go of her hand, so I walked with her to the kitchen where food was waiting for us. My tummy grumbled, and I wanted to sit down, but Mama turned around and headed for the stairs.

"Where are you going, Mama? You must eat something."

The Last Girl

"I just need to lie down a bit, Jacob. Go eat and come to me when you're done. And remember to wait for Papa before eating."

"Yes, Mama," I said, letting go of her hand. I shivered again as I watched her climb the stairs as if she were in pain.

"Leave her," Papa said, passing me. "Let's eat, boy." He entered the kitchen, sat at the head of the table, and without waiting for me, started eating. "Move it," he yelled, making me jump.

I ran to the kitchen and sat down. Picking up my fork, I scooped some egg and chewed slowly. I watched Papa while he ate, ensuring he finished his food first. The kitchen was quiet except for the clinking of our forks on the plate, and Papa doing that yucky sniffy thing he always did.

I drank some cold milk which cooled me from the inside. I picked up my toast and ate slowly, still watching Papa. When he finished his food, he said nothing to me. He just scraped the chair against the floor as he got up and left.

"Hurry, you have chores to do," Papa yelled as the screen door slammed.

I finished the rest of my food quickly and ran upstairs. I stood outside Mama's bedroom door with my hand hovering over the doorknob. "Mama, can I come in?" I asked.

"Yes," she said, barely above a whisper.

I turned the doorknob and opened the door.

"Come here, Jacob," Mama said, patting the bed beside her.

I entered her room, feeling nervous, and stopped on her side of the bed. She patted the bed again, and I jumped up to sit beside her. She was holding something I had never seen before. "What's this?" I asked.

"Our family photo album. Open it and see for yourself."

I took the album from her hands and placed it on the bed in front of me. I opened the first page.

"That's me and Papa on our wedding day," she said, turning the page, "and here are some of the family photos from the wedding."

"Why don't they visit?" I asked, turning the page with her. I didn't remember seeing anyone from these pictures.

Mama was quiet for a while. I glanced up when she said nothing and saw she had tears in her eyes.

"What's wrong?" I asked, reaching for the tear sliding down her cheek.

"There are good and bad things that happen in life," she said, swallowing hard. "And like all families, something happened in ours. It's a sensitive family matter and one reason we never see the family." She swallowed again. "You see, my boy, the night before I was supposed to get married, my unwelcome alcoholic uncle attacked me."

I sat up straighter and cocked my head to the side. "What do you mean? How did he hurt you?" I asked, not quite understanding what she meant.

"He hurt me badly." Mama seemed sad when she said that and didn't look at me, but she pointed to a picture of a man.

I stared at the photo of the uncle who had hurt Mama and, although I understood he had hurt Mama, I couldn't understand why I looked like him. I glanced up at Mama, wanting to ask her a question I didn't understand myself, instead I looked at the photo again.

"Why do I look like him?" I asked.

Mama started crying.

"Is he my real Papa?" I whispered as a tear fell from my

The Last Girl

eye, and then another. I wiped my eyes with my sleeve and sniffed.

Mama looked at me sadly. "My uncle was an awful man. He was in and out of jail for hurting others. And he wasn't supposed to visit, but then he just arrived, and my father couldn't send him away. I was awake late that night and bumped into him when I went to the kitchen, and then..." Mama left her words trailing and I could understand what may have happened to her.

"He's not a nice man for hurting you," I offered. I didn't know what else to say, what could I say. I was only ten.

"Papa and I still got married the next day like nothing had happened." She shrugged and glanced out the window. "Then after the trial, I found out I was pregnant. When you were born they did some tests and we found out you were not Papa's. We also found out that Papa couldn't have children, so we decided to keep you, even though Papa found it difficult." She smiled kindly, but there was something in her expression I didn't like.

I reached for her hand. She flinched, but then grabbed my hand and kissed it. "Everything worked out as it should, Jacob. It's all fine. So, you see, you must understand when Papa gets angry it isn't at you, it's the fact that he couldn't make you himself." She patted my hand and let me go.

"But why don't we see the family?"

"Oh, you know," Mama said, looking away again. "Bill fought with them because of everything that had happened and, well, nobody has attempted to reach out. So, it's just us." She glanced at me once more and wiped tears off her face. "Now run along. I need to rest."

I sat up on the bed, but she shook her head.

"Let me rest a bit and then, when I feel better, I'll give you a hug."

"Okay, Mama," I said, climbing off her bed and placing the photo album at the bottom of her side table. I glanced over my shoulder as I closed her door, and she was crying with the covers pulled up over her shoulders.

Mama didn't hug me that day.

Chapter Twenty-Seven

MAMA

Jack
2002

I stretched my back and waved dust out of my face again. The back of my neck started to itch as the Keychain in my hands made my fingers throb. I needed to see my *Keys*. Carefully, I rubbed each *Key* between my fingers; I would love them each one by one. I would provide them with the love that was never given to me. A love that was filled with compassion and kindness. And with each stroke of a *Key*, the itch slowly subsided.

The smooth surface of each *Key* as I moved my fingers between them helped the ache at the back of my head. I didn't want to remember any more memories. I'd had enough for one day, and the only thing that would help was if I saw another one of my *Keys*.

Chapter Twenty-Eight

THE MISSION - TUESDAY

Mike
2002

"Are you sure you want to do this?" I asked, parking on the side of the road near the long driveway that led to Jack's farmhouse.

Michelle glanced at me and smiled, but it didn't reach her eyes. "You know I have to do it."

"No, you don't. Let the police handle it." My eyes flitted from Michelle to the driveway and back to Michelle. "Let the detective handle it," I said softer, shaking my head. "He's already following leads, and he visited Jack. I'm telling you now he's on to Jack. Let him handle it."

"I understand what you're saying, but I can't allow the detective to handle my disappearance the way he handled Jessica's. Nah-ah," she grumbled. "I can't give up on my friend, Mike. I need to go in there and destroy that bastard." She pulled out a knife. I narrowed my eyes.

"Is that my mother's?"

"Yeah, sorry, you'll get it back when I'm finished with it."

"No, it's fine. Keep it. I'm sure you need it more than she does." I hated being in this position. Michelle was as stubborn as the next girl, but I wouldn't leave her to enter the monster's house. I sighed wearily and rubbed my eyes.

"If you don't hear from me by 5 p.m., go to the police station and tell the detective where I am."

"I don't like this. But I'll still go. What must I tell him?"

"Tell him everything."

"You do realize the detective can arrest us for falsifying events or tampering with stuff or whatever it's called. We will get into trouble."

"If I'm dead, nothing will happen to me, and besides, just tell him you knew nothing about it until now. That way, you can't get into trouble. Thanks, Mike," she said, staring into my eyes for a moment too long. "I appreciate everything you've done for us, and I'll see you soon."

Before I could answer, Michelle opened the door, jumped out of the car, and ran up the field alongside the driveway. She stuck to the shadows of the trees to avoid getting detected.

I turned the car around and slowly drove the dirt road back to town. My stomach twisted and turned, and I fought hard not to throw up.

Chapter Twenty-Nine

THE PHONE CALL

Detective Steve Campbell
2002

I'm going over the cold cases again, and the evidence we had stored, Officer Graham collected it and sent it for processing again. I wanted to find something that would lead us to Jack. Officer Graham was helping me with the case, and I was waiting for his return.

I flinch when the door swung open and slammed against the wall. Officer Graham stormed in, dumped the food on my table, and picked up the phone, hitting a button. He shoved the receiver into my face and nodded.

Who is it? I mouthed, but officer Graham's answer was almost hitting my jaw with the receiver. I took it out of his hands and answered, "This is Detective—" I could barely finish my words when a woman whispered into my ear.

"Detective, it's Michelle," she said.

"Michelle? Where are you?" I asked, glancing at Officer Graham with wide eyes.

"I'm in his house. Come quick."

"Whose house?"

"Jack's."

"Jack Haskins?" I asked, making sure we were on the same page.

"Yes," she said, barely above a whisper.

"Did he kidnap you?"

"Yes."

"Can you get out of the house?"

"No, hurry, he's looking for me. He's going to kill me. Please hurry." She slammed the phone down so hard my ear ached.

"We have to go," I said, standing, "see if there's anyone near Jack's farm. They need to enter Jack's house and look for her, then wait for us to arrive."

Officer Graham and I ran out of the office, with him calling on his radio for help.

Chapter Thirty

TAKE THAT

Michelle
2002

I couldn't believe I got inside Jack's house. I'm still in shock that I found an open window to climb through, but I'd lost my balance once I was through the window and smacked into the jar of cookies on the other side and watched in slow motion as it hit the floor, shattering.

I knew then that I had to hide somewhere, but I first needed Jack's home phone, which I found in the living room. After I made the call to the detective, I could only hope and pray he would send someone closer to see if I was really here and then he would get here himself, and soon.

I found a hiding spot behind the one couch and when I heard Jack storm upstairs from the basement in search of me; I clutched that phone against my chest and squeezed my eyes shut.

I could feel his gaze on me, even though I knew he

couldn't see me behind the couch. I knew I had to get downstairs when I heard him exit the living room and walk down the hallway.

Carefully, I placed the receiver back where it belonged and tiptoed out of the living room, saw Jack go into his room, and I bolted for the basement.

I was so scared the steps would creek, but to my relief they made little noise, and I hurried down the stairs.

Jack opened the basement door, then closed it again, and I heard the click as he locked the door. I knew he would come back; he knew I was here, or somebody was here, but I was sure he knew it was me.

He scared me, but I was here for a reason. I wanted my friend and would do everything I could to get her back. She was the reason I was putting my life at risk and would do so gladly; I knew she would do the same for me.

I wanted to call out to Jessica but hid in the corner of his dark basement and kept quiet. When Jack took long to return, I left the corner and went to the locker doors I remembered running through when I first escaped. I opened the doors but couldn't locate a mechanism that would open the back part.

A sense of dread hit me then. I had to get through to find my friend, but I knew I had to be patient. I had to wait for Jack to open the doors. Then I could find my friend.

When I heard the lock again, I bolted for the dark corner once more.

Chapter Thirty-One

UNWELCOME GUEST

Jack
2002

I touched the number 5 on the wooden door and closed my eyes as the memories of Olivia flashed in my mind's eye. She was one of my favorites. A blessing to me and the rest of my *Keys*.

"Enjoy lunch, my *Keys*." I turned and headed for the metal lockers when something upstairs fell over. My blood ran cold at the thought of someone entering my home.

I hurried through the metal lockers, closing them, and headed upstairs. I bolted into the kitchen, leaving the basement door open, stopping in front of the shattered jar of cookies on the floor. The only window in the kitchen was open, which I never opened, and the cookie jar had been on the opposite counter.

I turned the corner, and her floral scent caressed my

neck, and I smiled. I would never forget her scent. It seemed she had returned for more, and I would gladly give it to her.

I checked the living room, and her scent surrounded me there, too. I carefully walked down the hallway and checked the two rooms and then the bathroom. Nothing.

I stopped at the foot of the stairs and glanced up, shaking my head; she would never go up there. Then I turned toward the kitchen again and reached for the basement door and it was closed. I was sure I had left it open when I barged through earlier.

Carefully, I turned the handle and opened the door. Her floral scent was the strongest here. My smile stretched my face in two. I closed the door, locking it. I didn't want her escaping a second time. She could sit in the basement while I fetched something upstairs.

I ran to my old room upstairs, opened the closet, and pushed items away on the floor. Lifting the carpet to reveal the safe, I had moved from my father's room to mine. I retrieved the key from a sock and inserted it in the safe, turning the key, and it clicked open. Pushing keepsakes to one side, I grabbed the gun I'd taken from Michelle's handbag. There were other ways I could kill her, but it was poetic justice killing someone with their own gun, and I wanted her to feel pain quickly before it was over. I closed the safe, placed the key where it belonged, pulled the carpet back down, and stood.

Once downstairs by the basement door again, I slowly unlocked and opened the door. I had to be careful going down the stairs; I was sure Michelle had armed herself and was a little dangerous; the thought excited me and I adjusted myself.

My right hand squeezed the handle. I had powerful hands and would love to wrap my fingers around Michelle's neck and squeeze, to watch her light wink out of her eyes. But I knew she had something planned, and I had to be careful.

I smelled her scent in bursts as I traversed down the stairs. Sweat dripped down my back as adrenaline flooded my system.

"Do you realize you've broken into my home?" I said. My tone was deeper than usual. "I won't hesitate shooting anyone who dares coming onto my property without permission. The best part," I said, chuckling, "I don't even have to call the cops first. All I have to do is shoot." I stopped at the bottom of the stairs, my eyes adjusting to the darkness, and heard her soft-but-fast-raspy breathing. I imagined her chest moving up and down as she nervously took in air; her fight-or-flight responses kicking into effect.

Her floral perfume was everywhere with a hint of sweat. She was as excited as I was. I grinned. "I can hear you, Michelle," I taunted, moving along the far wall so that I had my front facing her danger.

I leaned forward and pulled on the cord dangling from the ceiling, illuminating the room. I rarely turned off the basement light; keeping it on for my lovely *Keys* so that they knew which direction my light for them came from since their rooms were always dark.

"Although it doesn't happen often, I love it when I get visitors. I have lots of *Little Keys* who have lost their way, and they all found me. Just like you, Michelle." I moved closer to the metal locker. "And I'd love for you to join my *Keys*, you never know, you might enjoy it."

I wrapped my knuckles across the metal lockers. "Won't you come out and show yourself?" My basement had three rows of standing shelves on the opposite side and against the walls were the washing machine and tumble dryer. And under the stairs stood the boiler, but there were dark nooks and crannies where she could squeeze her tight figure in.

"Come out, come out, wherever you are," I sang, moving along the wall heading toward the rows of shelves. Before I reached the shelves, a shadow under the stairs moved, catching my attention, and I stood still.

I changed direction and headed for the center of the basement. My smile reaching my eyes.

"I know what you did, you son of a bitch." The shadow darted forward between two of the shelves, her arms raised. She lunged for me, knocking my one side before returning to her shadows.

My shoulder burned, and I glanced down to look what was causing the pain. Staining my shirt bright red, my blood seeped into my clothing and dripped down my arm. The deep wound gushed blood, but I couldn't stop now to bandage myself and turned in the direction she'd gone down.

"That wasn't nice," I said, raising the gun. "Now be a darling and stand still for me. I'd like to take your picture."

She was quick. She lunged a second time, slicing the same shoulder.

"Bitch!" I groaned as more blood gushed. It was my right shoulder, making that arm weaker and my fingers unable to pull the trigger. As I lifted my head, she smacked into me, knocking me off my feet. My gun went clattering across the floor while she darted between the rows again.

"Dammit," I said, feeling a sting across my stomach. I scooted on my bum toward the gun and grasped it in my left, shaky hand. This woman was planning on slicing me to death, but as much as I was sure she wanted that, I couldn't allow it to happen. I took a moment to look at the wound on my stomach and was relieved it was superficial.

I needed to stop this girl before she hit a major artery. Leaning against the wall, I rested my arm with the gun on my knee and pointed it at a dark space between the shelves. I fired a few times, hoping one bullet would at least graze her body. When she didn't bolt out of the darkness, I used the last of my energy to stand up.

On shaky legs, I neared the darkest corner of the basement. With both hands holding the gun, I moved it where I heard a sound. I fired a few more shots, then stopped when something crashed to the ground and something metal clanked across the floor.

"No ways," I said, feeling blissful. "I didn't think it would be that easy." I traversed between the two shelves until I reached the wall and glanced left. "Yes," I said with joy. I grabbed her limp wrist and dragged her to the center of the basement. When I turned around, she sat up.

"Do you think I'll go down so easy?" she said, taunting me. Michelle reached for her chest and yanked off the vest, protecting her.

Not wanting to make the same mistake twice, I aimed for her head before she had time to realize I still had one bullet.

Chapter Thirty-Two

NURSING WOUNDS

Jack
2002

I opened the first aid kit and broke the zipper. Swearing under my breath, I threw all the contents out onto the floor and grabbed what I needed. Tearing the shirt from my body, I stared in anger at how that woman cut me. Blood poured down my arm, and I now needed to clean the floor from the basement to the bathroom.

After I washed the blood from my body, I added some gauze to my stomach to stop the bleeding while I cleaned the two wounds on my shoulder first with a generous blob of antiseptic. I used butterfly strips, Steri-Strips, to close the wounds and a plaster to keep everything in place. Then I did the same to the longer wound across my stomach.

Downing a few Tylenol tablets for pain, I pulled on clean clothing, and wiped down all the bloody spots and headed for the basement to collect Michelle and a shovel. I no longer wanted her near my *Keys*, she would only tarnish them, and the sooner she was in the ground, the better for me and my *Keys*.

I picked up the shovel and froze when the doorbell chimed. I dared not move, not wanting to make a sound, when the doorbell chimed a second time. "Shit," I whispered to myself.

They knocked and rang the doorbell a third time. When I heard footsteps moving farther away from me, down the steps, followed by the crunching of their shoes against the pebbles on the ground, I exhaled, the tension between my shoulders lessening.

When they started their vehicle and drove off, I lifted the shovel and headed for the back door. There was a spot in my greenhouse I could dig a hole, then when the evening was at its darkest, I would bury the girl.

Chapter Thirty-Three

NO ANSWER

Detective Steve Campbell
2002

Officer Graham drove the squad car while I sat in the passenger seat, calling all units to Jack's house when a call came through to my cellphone.

"Yes?" I asked, sounding grumpy.

"It's Officer Hank. I knocked on the suspect's door, but there's nobody home."

"Where are you now?"

"I left—"

"No, get back there," I yelled. "I need to make sure Michelle is alive and well. Get back."

"Yes, sir, I'm on my way back." Officer Hank hung up, and I slammed my fist on the dashboard.

"Hurry, Officer Graham," I yelled, "we need to get there now."

Chapter Thirty-Four

MIGHT AS WELL DIG TWO GRAVES

Jack
2002

I finished digging the hole, placed the shovel on the ground beside it, and went to the basement to fetch Michelle's body. Crouching near her body, I closed her eyes and shuddered. I hated when their eyes opened like that.

I brushed hair out of her face and scooped her up into my arms, wincing as I moved. The wounds felt like they were tearing open, forcing me to move her so that I was comfortable carrying her. As much as I would love to drag her across the floor by her hair, I wouldn't be a dick.

I climbed the steps when there was another knock at the door. I groaned inwardly and knew I had to answer, or they would blast through my front door. Instead, I went to the metal doors, opened the back, and entered the dark part.

"Hey, girls, don't be alarmed," I said, making sure my

Keys heard me clearly. "I'll be back to collect her. Nobody make a noise. You know the rules." I warned.

I closed the metal doors behind me, grabbed a few things from the shelves, and headed for the front door. The doorbell chimed again as I yanked the door open. "What?" I yelled, pulling the ear protectors off my head. "What's wrong? Was I making a noise?" I groaned, opening the door wider to peer outside. It was only one officer.

"Good afternoon, sir. May I come in?"

"No, now what are you doing here?" I yelled. The wounds on my shoulder burned from the sudden movements when I took the head protector off.

"Sorry to disturb you, but we received a distress call coming from inside your house, and I'd like to come inside and make sure there isn't a woman needing help."

"A woman?" I chortled. "Inside my house?" I thumbed behind me. "That's ridiculous."

"Please, sir, allow me access before SWAT arrives."

As much as I hated Michelle for calling the police from my house, I was happy she was dead in my basement and would take care of her body soon. But I had to manage this officer now; there was a stern warning in his tone, and I understood that if I blocked his access that things could get worse for me. I'd already stopped the detective from entering once before. If I did that again, I'd get more than just an accusation.

"Sure," I said, sighing loudly, opening the screen door, and standing to one side so that there was room for him to enter. "I've just been in the basement putting a fence together, so things are messy, but come inside and have a look around."

"Thank you," he said. "I'm Officer Hank and I shouldn't take too long." He smiled and entered my home.

He glanced at the spot where the mirror used to hang but said nothing, then he entered the living room, traversed down the hallway into the two rooms and then the kitchen.

I waited for him by the front door. The last thing I wanted to do was hang close to him while he had a look around. I leaned against the wall near the stairs, waiting for him to return from the kitchen. He glanced up at the cobwebs and dusty stairs.

"I don't use upstairs at all," I said when another car pulled up alongside the other cop car. "Who is that?"

"Detective Campbell," Officer Hank said, passing me and went outside. They spoke for a moment, then all three men headed my way.

"Jack," Detective Campbell said with disdain.

"Steve," I said with contempt.

"Mind if I poke around?"

"Not at all." I remained in my spot as the three men entered my home.

"I appreciate you allowing us to see if Michelle is here."

"There's nobody here but me, Steve."

"I'll be the judge of that, Jacob," the Detective said the name my parents had given me at birth. It was a name I despised, and the reason I changed my name to Jack was because I needed a new start. Jacob belonged to the rapist uncle, but Jack... Jack was me, and I was the *Master of my Keys*.

My lips curled over my teeth at the sound of that name, but quickly schooled my features. As much as I wanted to attack the detective and gouge out his eyes, the last thing I needed was to get arrested. Nobody would take care of my *Keys* if I was in jail. I counted to twenty and glowered at the man instead.

Steve entered with the other two trailing him, and they

searched everywhere. They had split up while I remained by the front door near the stairs.

Officer Hank neared me again, wanting to go upstairs.

"You're welcome to look, but I don't go up there anymore and I've lost the keys," I said with my hands in my pockets. My index finger rubbing my *Keys*.

Steve returned and thumbed behind him. "Go look in the basement with Officer Graham while I chat with Jack quickly."

I folded my arms across my chest and stared deadpan at him.

When the officer left us, Steve leaned against the balustrade. "I'd like to know why Michelle called from your house."

"Was it Michelle and was she really in my house?" I asked. "As you can see, there's nobody here but me." I pointed upstairs. "As I was telling the officer, you're welcome to go up there, but I don't know where the keys are. I haven't been up there after they murdered my parents."

Steve nodded once and glanced up stairs. "Where's your phone?"

"In the living room," I said.

Steve entered the living room, and I followed. He walked behind each chair and stopped near the couch and crouched.

A nervousness I hadn't felt earlier struck when I realized Michelle had been there when she called the detective.

Steve stood, holding something in his hand. "What did you do with her?" He moved around the couch and showed me strands of hair.

I narrowed my eyes. "What's that? Hair? From behind my couch." I shook my head. "You're clutching at straws, detective. And besides, you could've brought that in with you now. You aren't wearing gloves, and you were out of my sight. I don't trust you."

Anger flashed in the detective's eyes, and he pursed his lips; no doubt realizing his terrible mistake and stopping himself from lunging at me. I grinned.

"Detective," Officer Hank said as he approached, with the other officer behind him. "There's nothing down there, but he is building something."

"It's a chicken coop if you need to know." I smiled again, a little more smugly than before.

"Check the doors upstairs," Steve said, and Officer Hank did as requested. We waited in silence and Officer Hank was back quickly, dusting himself and sneezing.

"They're all locked up pretty tight," Officer Hank said.

Steve flinched and flicked a spider off Officer Hank's shoulder. The muscles along the detective's jaw ticked. "We'll be back," he said, moving toward the front door. "With a locksmith. I'd like to see what's behind those doors."

"Next time you're here, make sure you have a warrant. I'm done being generous, considering you barged in here accusing me of nonsense."

"I'll be watching you, Jack," he said, waving over his shoulder.

"I doubt that, Steve, because I'll lay charges of harassment if you or any other officer come near my property without just cause. I complied with your request earlier, and you found nothing. Don't test my patience."

Steve turned around as the other two officers passed him and there was something in his eyes; rage maybe, possibly hate.

"And how's that lovely wife of yours?" I asked. "I heard

she hasn't been feeling well." I locked the screen door, and slowly closed the door in his face.

"You mother—" he started, but the other officer grabbed him by his arms and pulled him away. He continued mumbling something I had no interest in hearing, but he understood what I was getting at. Steve wasn't stupid, and he knew I had been at his house, and I hoped now he understood I wasn't to be messed with, and I would go after his wife if he continued pestering me.

I locked the front door and relaxed. My right hand shook and the wounds on my shoulder burned. I entered the kitchen, locked that door, and bolted all the windows shut. I didn't want anyone gaining entrance again.

I entered the living room and peered through the curtains, noting their vehicles were gone but suspected they had parked nearby. Just in case.

I needed to transport Michelle's body in something instead of carrying her over my shoulder; that would look suspicious and cause for concern. If she were in my wheelbarrow, then it looked like I was just moving sand from my basement to the greenhouse.

Chapter Thirty-Five

DILEMMA

Detective Steve Campbell
2002

"I hate that guy," I yelled, smashing my fist on the steering wheel. As selfish as this sounded but I had forgotten about Michelle because Alice was my priority. I needed to keep her safe now that Jack had threatened her life. I had to move her to a place where Jack couldn't find her.

"I need someone to take my wife to the station," I said, but then thought about it. Alice would hate that, and it would scare her; I would have to do it myself. Perhaps now was the perfect time to take her to hospital; that would be the safest place and she could receive the care she needed. I exhaled loudly.

"Take a breath," Officer Graham said. "I've only interacted with him on a few occasions, and he was pleasant. But that," he thumbed behind him, "that was creepy, and most likely our suspect. But we need to do this correctly," he jerked his chin toward the farmhouse, "he knows we're on to him, so he'll be more careful. We can watch him from a distance and hopefully unnerve the bastard. Let's get the warrant. And I'd suggest taking your wife to nearby friends or family just to be safe. One never knows," he said, the last part looking at me.

"She needs medical care," I said above a whisper. "While Officer Hank gets the warrant, you stay here and watch the house, and I'll take care of Alice."

He nodded. "Absolutely."

"Will you be okay without a car?"

"Sure, I'll call if he goes anywhere." He opened the car door and before he closed it, he leaned in. "I know it's hard, but don't let him mess with you. I'll be right here when you get back." He closed the door and knocked twice on the roof.

I nodded, turned the car around and drove slowly down the driveway, watching the farmhouse get smaller in the rearview mirror.

Chapter Thirty-Six

TO THE RESCUE

Mike
2002

I paced up and down the hallway waiting for the big hand to hit the five and Michelle still hadn't called.

"You need to go," Mom said, peering over her glasses at me. "That silly girl has gotten herself into trouble."

"Shh, Ma, don't say it out loud," I grumbled and grabbed my keys. "I'll see you soon." I hated myself for allowing Michelle to enter that man's house, but nothing would've stopped her. But I hated myself even more for not stopping Jessica. Then none of this would've happened. Unfortunately, I couldn't go back in time and had to deal with the consequences for the rest of my life.

"Tell the new detective I said hi."

I rolled my eyes. Once a flirt, always a flirt. "Bye, Ma."

I drove the short distance to the police station, parked my van, and entered. There were people running around like something major had happened. Someone shouted as they passed papers to the next officer. I headed straight to reception.

"Hi, can I speak with Detective Campbell, please?"

The receptionist peered at me over her thinly rimmed glasses. "You'll have to wait a bit, sir," she said, and continued working. "The detective is busy with another case."

I had a sneaky suspicion it was about Jack. I heard someone yell about kidnappings and knew they were on to something. "Please," I said with determination. "Can you tell him that Michelle was at Jack's house and she hasn't called me? She said if I didn't hear from her that the cops needed to go to Jack's house now."

The receptionist raised her eyebrows, her mouth wide open. "They were just there," she said, picking up her receiver. "Detective..." The receptionist started and told him everything I'd said with me chiming in now and then with additional information. She was quiet for a moment while she listened to the detective, then hung up.

"Well, what did he say?" I asked, eager to find out.

"Once they have the warrant, they'll search his property and hopefully arrest him." She smiled.

"But she needs them now," I yelled, and stopped myself from slamming my fist on the counter. "She might not have until tonight. She might be dead, or Jack could have locked her up in a dirty place. Michelle had said there's a secret level below the basement." I couldn't believe I'd forgotten about that. "Tell him, pick up the phone again and tell him that there's a secret door somewhere in his basement, and the other girls are down there."

"Okay, okay, I'll let him know. Is there anything else before I do?" she asked and picked up the receiver again.

I stood back and exhaled. "No, that's it. But he must go to her now."

"He will the moment he can. Leave me your details and go home. We don't need civilians going over there, so promise me you'll go home and wait for the detective to call you."

I raised my hands in mock surrender. "Yeah, of course."

I wrote my details while she spoke with the detective again and left.

Chapter Thirty-Seven

TO BURY A BODY

Jack
2002

I eyed the detective's car narrowly and was relieved when he drove down the driveway. "Bye, asshole," I mumbled to myself, and headed for the basement.

A few years after my parents were dead, I had renovated parts of the farmhouse. One item I had removed was the bulkhead doors that led into the basement because I didn't want another entrance or exit into that room. I needed to restrict all access in case one of my *Keys* escaped. At the moment, I wished I had one because now I had to pick up Michelle's corpse again and carry her up a flight of stairs and into the kitchen.

My shoulders strained, but I got Michelle into the wheelbarrow I'd wheeled into the kitchen. The back door stood open, and all I had to do was cross the yard and get into the greenhouse. The sun had already set, and the moonless sky graced me with its darkness.

I turned off the outside lights and maneuvered the wheelbarrow down the steps and path toward the greenhouse. I pushed the wheelbarrow through and stopped to look around.

When I was content nobody was nearby, I closed the greenhouse door behind me and pushed Michelle along the narrow path through my dying sunflowers until I reached the hole waiting for her.

When I reached the spot near my pink sunflower, I tipped the wheelbarrow, and she landed in her new home with a solid thud sound. I picked up the shovel and covered her with dirt. I first ensured no body part was sticking out at an odd angle before closing the hole.

Once done, I leaned on the shovel and stared down at her grave. Relieved I finally put her in her place, I smiled. I had come too far and for so long to have it all taken away from me by some girl who thought she could rescue her friend. I snorted. She wished she was the last girl; there were plenty more girls for me to enjoy.

I patted the sand flatter with the shovel, placed it in the wheelbarrow and pushed it toward the greenhouse exit. I closed the glass door behind me and pushed the wheelbarrow around the house and left it inside the barn.

Slowly I traversed down the driveway to see if there were any cars but saw none. There was some movement on my right but chalked it up to the shadows playing tricks on me and headed back toward the house.

Chapter Thirty-Eight

BACK TO NORMAL

Jack
2002

Once back inside the safety of my house, I locked all the doors again and switched on some lights. My clothing was dirty and the wounds on my shoulder and stomach started aching again. I undressed and climbed under the shower. The hot water was both wonderful and painful; it also washed away everything I hated about the day; the girl trying to ruin everything in my life, and that nosy detective.

Still sitting with just a towel around my waist, I cleaned and dressed the wounds. The wound on my stomach was doing ok, but the two gashes on my shoulder had torn open slightly and probably needed stitches, but the butterfly strips I had would suffice.

I pulled on fresh clothing and grabbed all the dirty washing that needed cleaning and headed for the basement to the washing machine. Once I loaded the clothing, I switched on the machine and grabbed an old rag and started looking for any marks Michelle may have left behind. I entered the metal doors, ensuring I left nothing incriminating behind.

"Goodnight my lovelies," I said to my *Keys*, "dream of me as I'll dream of you." I closed the metal doors, feeling elated the day had ended on such a positive note.

That girl was gone.

My *Keys* were still in their places, and the detective did not know what to do next.

Tonight, I would enjoy a glass of wine. The last time I had any wine was after my parents had died. I smiled at the fond memory… and it felt like yesterday I had been blessed.

Chapter Thirty-Nine

THE WAIT

Jack
2002

The back of my neck itched and the more I scratched, the more it itched. I paced up and down the hallway while rubbing my *Keys* between my fingers.

I stopped by the living room curtains and parted them slightly. The moonless night bathed my land in darkness, and I'd switched off all the lights in the house except the light in the kitchen. They were out there, watching me, waiting. And I would wait here and watch them approach.

Something sounded downstairs.

My *Keys*.

A terrible thought came to mind. If something happened to me, what would happen to my *Keys*?

I needed to make sure someone would take care of my lovelies; but who and how. The thought of someone else touching them with their sticky fingers left me feeling queasy. But if they hurt me, what would happen to *Them*... I couldn't finish my thought.

No, I thought, shaking my head. Nothing would happen to me or my *Keys*. Nobody was taking them away from me. I was going nowhere.

Glancing outside, I had to keep them away from my house and away from my *Keys*.

Chapter Forty

ARMED AND DANGEROUS

Detective Steve Campbell
2002

"Hey, my love," I said as I entered our room. Alice was still in bed, staring out into nothing.

I reached for the covers and pulled them back. Alice was wearing my pajamas, making her look tiny and fragile. I smiled and sat on the bed.

"I've called the doctor, and he's waiting for you." I leaned forward and kiss her cheek.

"Why?" she asked, blinking up at me.

I already sensed fear from her and was glad I was the one to take her instead of someone she didn't know. They would've frightened her to tears.

"It's just a routine checkup," I said with an upbeat tone in my voice. There was no way I could tell her that a deranged man who had kidnapped women had targeted her. She would never leave our house.

"Okay," she said and slowly sat up.

I stood and reached for her hands. "I've already packed you an overnight bag, and the doctor said you can stay in your pajamas. You would've gotten changed in them, anyway. At least now you'll arrive in comfort."

She giggled, and it warmed my heart. I loved her giggle. I loved her. Alice stepped into her slippers, and we descended the stairs. I picked up her bag, locked the front door, and got into the car.

Before I turned the key to start the ignition, I watched Alice relax in the seat and was overcome with sadness; for all those women Jack had hurt; I would not exact revenge on him, but I was going to get him off the streets so that he couldn't hurt anyone else.

"I got it!" I yelled, running through the station, and called Officer Hank to come with me. Two other officers joined us in their cars, and we headed for Jack's house.

"Is Officer Graham still there?" Officer Hank asked.

"Yep, he says nothing has happened that he could tell, but all the lights are off except for the kitchen."

"Do you think he knows we're on to him?"

"Definitely," I said, taking a corner a little too fast and slowed down. "And if he doesn't know, he'll find out soon."

It relieved me to know that Alice was safe, and nobody knew where she was. Her doctor had admitted her into a private ICU room to ensure her safety. It left me with only one worry; to find Michelle and Jessica alive.

The drive to Jack's house was filled with quiet anticipation. My shirt clung to my body even though it was cold out, and although I'd been in situations like this before when I was in Las Vegas, they were always different.

I slowed the car. In the distance, a dark shadow waved their arms. As the headlights touched his legs, I knew it was Officer Graham flagging us down. I stopped the car a short distance from him.

"I didn't want him seeing the car lights and running off," Officer Graham said, huddling into his jacket. January was our coldest month, and it had snowed again.

"You want to get inside and warm again?" I asked, noting his lips were blue. "Sorry, I didn't think it would get this cold so quickly."

"It's ok," Officer Graham said, climbing into the back seat. His teeth were chattering as he sat down and blew into his hands. "It was only three hours. I'll live." He smiled.

"Did you see anything else?"

"Nah, after you left, I took a walk around his property and tried to stay out of sight. I saw little, but he is still in there. It's just awfully dark."

"We have the warrant," I said, waving the piece of paper, "and I want Jack to get a fright when he sees us. So before I drive up there, check your weapons and put a vest on. I brought extra." I thumbed toward the trunk.

The other two officers pulled up behind us and waited.

When everyone was ready, we took the slow drive up, and I parked in front of his house. The headlights illuminated his front door, and I kept them on with the car idling. We climbed out of the car and approached the house.

"Jack!" I yelled. "I have a warrant with me this time." I waved the piece of paper in the air. "Let us in."

"I can't do that, Steve," Jack yelled from somewhere inside his house.

"Why not?"

"You'll ruin everything."

"Jacob!" I called him by his former name just to irk him. There were two ways I could've done this; be nice so that he opened the door or anger him. I had already tried both approaches, but I had come to realize that Jack just didn't like me, so either way would've yielded the same result. Admittedly, calling him Jacob was in poor taste, but I wanted him to come outside and speak with me; I wanted him angry and to say something we could use against him.

"Open, buddy, it's the law," I said. "You don't want me to call for backup."

He didn't respond, but I heard him stomping around inside of his house.

"Was Kate your first?" I yelled. "What did she do to you? I heard you guys were the best of friends." I stepped closer. "Oh, and we got the results from your parent's murder. You were the only one there that evening, weren't you?" I neared the veranda steps. "It seems wherever I look there you are, Jack. The last one to see Kate alive. The last one to see your parents alive. And all those women. Why?" It was a rhetorical question, but I had to ask. I had to find out what made this guy tick. "And you were the last one to see Michelle; the night of her disappearance and today. I can't help but think you are the cause of everything, Jack. Open before this gets ugly."

I sensed his dark gaze, and he was most probably trying to kill me with it, but it wouldn't happen. We could storm his house and fight him there or he could come out here. Either way, we would get him.

We climbed the steps of the veranda when a door slammed. I froze and turned to the others. "Back door?" They nodded. I ran out in front of them and around the house. I saw someone with a torch running away and down the hill. "Stay here and find the women. And call an ambulance." I called out and ran after Jack.

I grabbed my flashlight from my duty belt and switched it on. My heart thundered in my chest as sweat peppered my forehead. I ran in the direction I thought he went but couldn't see his flashlight anywhere. Snow continued falling as I tried to see which direction he'd gone in when my light struck footsteps in the snow.

Chapter Forty-One

ON THE RUN

Jack
2002

I saw a trailer for Minority Report that's set to release sometime this year and in there Tom Cruise said that everybody ran. Whether one was guilty or innocent, we all ran. It's part of our fight-or-flight instinct. Mine was to run as well, and I had to get the detective away from my *Keys*. He would only ruin them with his tainted touch, and me standing around allowing them to take me away was not an option, either. I had to evade capture so that I could return after the police had left and rescue my *Keys*. I hoped they didn't know about my secret basement.

I ran along the old hiking trail I used when I was a kid and thought I would've forgotten it, but luckily the vegetation had grown little in the area and there was little snow. During the day in the summer months, this was a lovely place to walk; it took one right around the mountain. My family was very lucky to have bought this piece of land with the mountain for our backyard.

It would be easy to lose the detective here; there were lots of twists and turns. If one didn't know where they were going, they could end up on the other side and farther away. Which I hoped the detective would do.

I took the path on the left, then carefully backed up, stepping in the same footsteps. Then I walked down the path on the right and headed for the mountain.

When I reached the stream, I slowed down. For the first time in ten minutes, I could catch my breath, glancing over my shoulder to see if he was behind me and in the distance I caught sight of a flashlight moving up and down at a steady pace as the detective approached. I smiled when he went completely off the path, following the fake path I'd taken.

Chapter Forty-Two

THE CHASE

Detective Steve Campbell
2002

I followed his footsteps until I came to a fork in the road. Judging from the footsteps going in both directions, it was impossible he had gone down both paths.

My right knee pained from all the running, and I stopped for a second to rub the aching area. When my lungs no longer burned, I glanced to the side and saw the path veered to the right and closer to the mountain while the path on the left went down the hill.

Something up ahead caught my attention, and I narrowed my eyes. The light winked out, and I was sure it was Jack turning off his flashlight down there. I glanced at the path on the left and was unsure about it, but I walked a few steps down in that direction while watching the speck I'd seen, and it moved.

Jack.

Jack was down there. The speck disappeared, and the shadow moved farther to the right.

No. This was the wrong path, and I backtracked, taking the path on the right instead.

Chapter Forty-Three

DO OR DIE

Jack
2002

I could no longer see Steve's flashlight, which told me he had backtracked and gone down my path and would reach me soon. I cursed under my breath as I followed the narrow path along the cliff's edge. The stream flowed down below, but once I reached it and crossed to the other side, I could escape through the trees. There were a few houses there and then the main road. I could flag a car down and get out of here and come back after the cops had left.

My foot slipped, and I grabbed the rock, slicing my palm. I swore and bit my lip, ensuring no sound came out. My shoulder ached as the butterfly strips pulled tightly. I slowly stepped down and jumped onto the bank, the water lapping against my shoes. I shivered. Snow fell around me, and the sight was beautiful for what it was; Mother Nature doing her best to keep us hooked on her.

This part of the stream was the shallowest, and I crossed to the other side. The icy water struck my legs, making them ache. I turned off my flashlight and waited until my eyes adjusted to the darkness. I stood on the other side of the stream and watched for movement on the hill.

An owl hooted above me. The sound of the moving water was hypnotic, but then the sound of a heavy man crushing vegetation with his boots angered me.

Steve followed the narrow path and was heading my way sooner than I thought. He was moving quickly for a man with a knee injury.

Now that my eyes had adjusted to the darkness, I ran as quickly as I could. My running had set off the detective, and he, too, started running. He cursed and swore as he crossed the river. I smiled. I had a good head start.

The vegetation was short, and I could make out the various dark shapes that were bushes or trees, but knew I had to take it easy or I'd fall. I slowed down to a stroll and grabbed my flashlight. I doubted the detective could see where I was, even with my flashlight on, but I needed to see where I was going.

I just turned it on and moved the light when my cold, wet foot struck a stone and I fell forward. My flashlight went flying to the right. I fell forward, my hands hitting rock, followed by my knees and shins. Bones crunched, my fingers snapped, and pain shot up my legs.

I groaned as I sat up and turned around so I could assess the damage. My flashlight was a distance away from me and I couldn't move until I saw what was going on with my shin. I pulled up my right wet pant leg and felt my shin; something was sticking out of my skin, and I painfully assumed it was part of the bone that had splintered. There

The Last Girl

was no way I could walk out of here unaided and needed to find a walking stick of some sort.

Footsteps sounded up ahead, and they were closing in on me. I swore under my breath. I opened and closed my fingers, and my knuckles were just scraped. My left knee was just bruised. I felt the rock I was sitting on, and my right leg had hit a part of the rock that had a protruding point. No wonder my shin got hurt.

I glanced around for something I could use to help me walk, but there was nothing; only bushes and rocks.

The detective's flashlight moved vigorously from left to right and left again as he jogged in my direction.

I found long broken branches that were thick enough, tore parts of my t-shirt, and made a splint. I bit into bark and bound the wood against my lower limb. The pain shot up my leg and it felt like I wanted to pass out.

Steve stopped walking and searched the ground with his flashlight.

I froze.

"Give up, Jack," Steve said, and started walking again. "There's no escaping."

I made a second knot and tried to stand. Pain shot up my leg, and I fell back onto the rock. I needed to find something I could use to help me stand.

"You're surrounded," Steve yelled, coming closer. "There's nowhere to hide."

I sighed wearily; I couldn't run away from him and because of my fresh wounds, I could barely move. There was nothing I could do but face the detective.

I grabbed the gun from my jacket pocket and aimed it at him. My shoulder burned, forcing me to hold it with both hands. Sweat dripped down the sides of my face, and I hurried to wipe it out of my eyes.

His dark shadow moved. He pointed his flashlight down and all I saw was the light on the ground. In the distance, red and blue lights struck the mountain. There were more of them now. My chest squeezed.

My *Keys*.

There were more of them to search my house. More of them to hurt my *Keys*. I had to kill the detective and go back home to save my *Keys*.

Steve edged closer.

His flashlight moved on the ground, closing in on me. I tried to move my foot away, but I wasn't fast enough and his light struck my shoe. I raised my arm again, aiming it at the thick darkness. The light moved up my leg, chest, and then my hands and eyes.

"Drop your weapon," Steve said, his tone sending a chill down my spine, and something clicked. "I will shoot. Now lower your weapon."

Slowly, I lowered my weapon. The flashlight dropped slightly, and Steve closed the gap. As he got to me, I raised my arm again and pulled the trigger at the same time he did.

Pain erupted in my chest. Something wet dripped down my stomach and pooled in my lap. The detective fell to his knees near my feet and raised his weapon again. I narrowed my eyes and raised my weapon but was too late. Steve pulled the trigger before me, and all I saw was darkness.

Chapter Forty-Four

HOUSE OF HORRORS

Detective Steve Campbell
2002

I felt joy on my hike back to Jack's farmhouse and I almost had tears in my eyes. It relieved me that Jack would no longer be hurting anyone ever again. The paramedics carried Jack's body to the ambulance and would transport it to the medical examiner's office. And I was grateful I wore my vest, protecting my chest from Jack's bullet; it would leave a bruise but it would heal.

Officer Graham waved me over. "You've got to see this, detective." He shuddered. "I've seen nothing like this before."

The hike to the stream and back had exhausted me, but adrenaline continued coursing through my veins, giving me the energy to continue. I had to see the girls and make sure they were okay. I pulled on those blue paper booties and a pair of gloves and followed Officer Graham inside the house.

"Would you like to see upstairs or downstairs first?" he asked.

"Upstairs," I said, needing to know what was upstairs first. Jack had been so secretive about the locked rooms there.

I ascended the steps, waving dust out of my face. The lights were on everywhere and I could make out stains on the seventies wallpaper with it tearing in most of the corners of the hallway.

James, the technician, was taking pictures in one room. The sound of the camera clicking made me flinch each time. We stopped outside a room, and I stared numbly inside.

"Have you ever seen anything like this before?" Officer Graham asked.

I shook my head. "Never," I said, entering the room. "Do you think he dug them up?"

"Definitely, and probably soon after their funeral. They've been rotting away in their sheets for years," James said, pulling the sheet away from their bodies, and chunks of dried flesh with it.

Officer Graham gagged and exited the room.

I stared at the mummified bodies of Jack's parents and whistled. "Talk about disturbed."

"You should look at the other rooms then tell me which is worse."

"No ways," I said. "What could be worse than this?"

"You'll see," James said.

"Maybe open a window or something," I said, waving my hand in front of my face, "it smells in here."

I left James to finish his job and entered the next

bedroom; it was Jacob's bedroom, frozen in the 1970s. There were wooden toy blocks scattered everywhere on the floor, an old scruffy teddy bear on a knitted blanket on his bed, and a toy train on a shelf. The shelves were clean, and the bedside table was dust free. I wondered whether Jack came up here often to play with his toys or laid on his bed.

I opened his closet and found clothing for a six-year-old boy. Moving the hangers to one side, I flinched when I came across a doll hanging from the rail. I moved the hangers again to cover the doll and kicked something with my foot. The carpet had lifted, and I crouched, pulling the carpet up, revealing a safe that needed a key to open.

I searched the shelves for the key, pushing items around when something clanged against the side. I reached for the sock and found it. Inserting it into the safe, I turned the key, and it clicked open.

I pulled each item out slowly; a box full of ladies' jewelry that could've belonged to the girls, a box of diamond earrings that may have been his mother's, lots of cash, bonds, and bank statements. I whistled. He was very rich.

I opened the chest of drawers, and it was just socks, some books, and more toys. Once I had finished in his room, I told James what I'd found in the safe and he said he'd look once he finished in the parent's room.

Then, I entered the third bedroom. The smell of dried blood greeted me and I swallowed hard. My eyes bounced across the walls and floor. Blood drained from my face, leaving my skin cold and my palms damp inside the gloves.

"Scary, isn't it?" James said from the doorjamb. "One crazy dude."

"I'll say," I said, not wanting to look away from the

carnage. "Have you taken pictures and samples of everything yet?"

"Yep, I left the parents for last. Thanks for finding the safe. I'll go there now."

"How can anyone live like this?"

"I think he loved it. He wanted it like this."

I shook my head in disgust. Jack had painted the entire room in blood; most of it was old but some of it seemed fresh. There wasn't a single section of the room not covered in blood. It smelled like an abattoir cleaned with organs. And in the center of the room was an oval carpet with a recliner and a wooden table beside it. The carpet didn't look like a normal carpet; it was various shades of black, brown, and dirty white. I stepped inside the room, the dried blood cracking beneath my booties, and crouched, touching the carpet, and regretted it the moment I realized what it was.

"Jesus," I said, bouncing back up.

"Hair," James said, standing beside me. "Human hair."

I stared wide eyed at him and gagged, swallowing hard. I'd hardly eaten today, but I would still throw up anything left in my stomach.

"I don't think I can see any more."

"Wait until you get downstairs."

"Do I want to know?" I asked, even though I did.

Once I was downstairs near the open front door, I took in deep breaths before going to the basement. I felt lightheaded but needed to continue with the investigation.

Someone was vomiting outside near a car.

I turned around and headed for the kitchen; the sooner I got this over with, the sooner I could see Alice. I needed her after the night I was having.

I reached the basement and glanced around, not seeing

anything. Then Officer Graham came through the metal locker.

"Secret passage," he said, thumbing behind him. I remembered Mike had mentioned metal lockers were an entrance to another section of the basement. There were lights on inside the room, illuminating the soil and wooden beams.

Dread filled my veins, but I neared the metal lockers and stepped through. It felt like I'd stepped into an episode of the Twilight Zone. The smell of wet soil wafted in the air along with another stink I couldn't quite place. Old wooden doors and walls lined the dirt hallway. There were lights on everywhere, so I was grateful we had brought our own and had set them up.

"Here's the key to open each of the rooms," Officer Graham said, dangling a keychain in his gloved hands.

"Are all the doors unlocked?"

"They are now," he said, still pale.

I approached the first door and pushed it open. There was already one of our lights inside, illuminating the space. Soil. A dirty mattress. A bucket. An empty bottle of water. The smell. I blocked my nose as my stomach turned. What caught me off guard was there was no woman to rescue. Nobody was calling out to us. I assumed the women were here, desperately trying to escape.

But the room was empty except for those few items and a mattress, and the item on top of the mattress. "Is that in every room?" I asked.

"Yep, the same items," Officer Graham said sadly. "A mattress, a bucket, and an empty water bottle."

"Where are the women?" I asked as I exited the room to check the others. They were all the same. Dirty floor with a mattress and each smelled terrible, and on top of each mattress was a blue floral dress neatly laid out, waiting for someone to pull it on. "And does that look like the dress Jack's mom is wearing?" I thumbed at the ceiling.

"Yep," Officer Graham said.

I was about to leave when he called me back.

"There's something else, detective," he said, entering the first room. "There's more." With his boot, he pushed the mattress to one side.

"What's that?" I asked, crouching. I pinched the mattress between my thumb and index finger and raised it. "Damn," I said, not quite believing this. The higher I raised the mattress, the more it stank; beneath the mattress in a small hole were the skeletal remains of a woman, I assumed. Her clothing clung to her boney figure.

"Awful," Officer Graham said, "just awful. So glad that man is dead."

Standing up, I shook my head. "I can't believe it. I thought they were alive." Sweat dripped down my face and I used my arm to wipe it out of my eyes. "What about Jessica and Michelle?"

"No Michelle, but this one we think is Jessica. She's the only one missing a top, and she has more flesh on her bones, and her face vaguely looks like her photo," he said and exited the room and entered a room right at the back. "We counted twenty rooms and they're filled with the same type of mattress and blue floral dress."

"Twenty?" I asked, my voice raised. "We need to widen our search to include the other victims."

"Yep," he said, waving me inside.

I stood beside him and stared down at the shallow grave with Jessica in the fetal position, her head shaved. I cringed, remembering the carpet made of hair.

"This place is a house of horrors," I said, stepping outside of the room, desperately needing fresh air.

"You can say that again," Officer Graham said, wiping his sweaty face. "It's over and now we can give their families peace of mind. They now know where their daughters are. It's sad news, but at least they'll know."

I nodded my agreement; grateful the streets would be safer for a while longer.

Chapter Forty-Five

ALICE

Detective Steve Campbell
2002

I wrapped my knuckles on the doorjamb. Alice turned around and smiled. It was the smile I'd fallen in love with all those years ago when we first met at school. The smile I loved even more when she walked down the aisle. And the smile today reminded me why I loved her still.

"Are you ready?" I asked, stepping inside her room to take her bag.

"Yep, I can't wait to go home."

"Me, too. I've missed you."

Alice had been in hospital for three days so that the doctors could assess her mental and physical wellbeing. She had improved so much that she was ready to leave today.

I walked past her bag and reached for her, cupping her face, and kissing her gently. She melted in my arms as I held her tightly. It felt so good having her back.

I ended the kiss and let go. "You look great, my love," I said, grabbing her bag and holding my hand out for her.

She took my hand in hers and stood by my side. "I feel so much better," she said, relaxing against my side. "Let's go home."

Our car ride home was quick, and we spoke about everything; from my case to her little "getaway".

"Thank you for not giving up on me," she said, placing her handbag on the table near the front door. She sighed and went to the kitchen. "Coffee?"

"Yeah, sure," I said, dropping her bag near the door. "Why would I ever give up on you?" I asked, feeling confused.

"Well," she said, shrugging, "I wasn't myself for a very long time."

"You had gone through a lot, honey, and why would I just desert you. I'm not cold or cruel. You're my wife and I love you. I'll do anything and everything I can to help you."

Her smile brightened her face. She poured me a cup of coffee and leaned against the counter. Her eyes darted to something behind me. I turned around to see what it was and froze. I'd been so busy with the case, I'd hardly been home, that I hadn't thrown the pink sunflower away.

"What's that?" she asked, sipping her coffee.

"It's nothing. I think Jack dropped it off to scare me—"

"Does he grow them?"

I looked up at her, my mouth opening in a surprised O. "Dammit," I said, reaching for my cellphone.

"What is it?" she asked with concern.

"We never found Michelle's body and because that house was so horrific, nobody bothered checking the sunflowers in the greenhouse."

"Do you think he buried her body there?"

"Yeah," I said convincingly. "I do."

We stood around the freshly dug up site, staring down at Michelle's twisted body in the ground. The girl was infuriating, but all she wanted to do was find her friend. She wanted to find Jessica before Jack hurt her, but it was too late.

Too late for any of Jack's girls. It relieved me that Michelle would be his last girl.

We had found more missing women than we had thought, and we had notified most of the parents. And we had Jack; his body was still in the morgue. He would hurt no woman again. And that alone brought me comfort.

I did my best and I could kick myself for not doing more. I could only hope the next case I would solve before there was another victim.

Bonus Chapter

THEN THERE WAS ONE

Jack - 21 years old
1987

I wiped my nose with a crumpled tissue and sneezed. The wind blew dust everywhere, irritating my sinuses. I fixed my black tie and pulled my black jacket straight. I stood silently beside people who had known my parents; people I didn't care to speak to but had to.

They turned on the casket lowering system and I watched as both coffins entered the ground at the same time. It was silent. The two men ensuring everything worked correctly worked constantly. I imagined one side getting stuck and the casket tipping on one side, with Papa falling out. I smiled, then quickly schooled my features, and glanced around at the people.

Once both coffins were in the ground, they removed the little curtain from the frame and dismantled it piece by piece. The priest said something and most of the people left to stuff their faces with triangle sandwiches and tea.

I reached for the family photo they had used of Papa and Mama, who wore her blue floral dress; she always looked so pretty in that dress. I was part of that photo, but they had cut me out for obvious reasons.

I missed Mama. The emotion never lasted, but today I missed her. Occasionally she had touched me gently, had spoken a kind word, or had made me my favorite sandwich. It wasn't often she showed tenderness and the softness of her voice never lasted. She always looked out for Papa. He never approved of her doing anything nice for me.

It was then that I realized Mama was always nice to me when she wore her blue floral dress. I ensured they buried her in her favorite dress and, although she was dead, she had looked lifelike in her coffin.

The cut above my eye itched, and the stitches in my back pulled tight against my skin. I had wedged the knife between bricks in the basement and fell back into it. I was glad it missed a lung, or I would've struggled, but it all worked out in the end. And the Sheriff had believed the story I had given. There were no follow-up questions or wanting me to take them through that night again.

Bludgeoning my parents was easy. The hard part was where to hide the hammer. I buried it in the far, dark corner of the basement. Nobody would find it. I wrapped it in my clothing and walked naked to the bathroom, where I showered and climbed back into my pajamas, then hit, and stabbed myself.

Before their demise, I had stood at the foot of their bed and had watched them sleep. Papa had snored while Mama was silent; I almost thought she had stopped breathing by herself.

The Last Girl

I had first slit their throats, Papa's was much deeper than Mama's, and then I had hit them a few times with the hammer. The knife was back in the kitchen; carefully cleaned.

Then I ran through the house, first in a pair of my father's boots and then with my bloody feet so that it seemed too chaotic for them to decipher what had really gone on.

When I was content everything was in place, I ran to our neighbor, who was a couple of miles away. By the time I reached her, my feet were bloody and raw and the wounds on my back and head were bleeding profusely, and I was about to pass out. Mrs. Oxford screamed so loudly it was music to my ears.

"Jacob," Sheriff Adams said, pulling me out of my thoughts and grabbing my shoulder. "How are you feeling?"

I glanced at him with mournful eyes. "Not great," I said sadly. "Have you found anything yet?"

"Not yet, my boy," he said, not looking me in the eye. "And there's nothing else you can remember?"

"No?" I shook my head and averted my eyes. "I can't believe I left them to be slaughtered. If I'd stayed and fought him off, maybe they could still be alive."

"It's not your fault. You had to get out of there," he said, patting my shoulder. "And if you stayed to fight him, all three of you could be in the ground right now. So don't beat yourself up. You did the right thing running to your neighbor."

"What about Mama's jewelry? Could you find it at any of the pawn shops?"

The sheriff shook his head, still not looking me in the eye. "No, but we'll keep an eye out." He was quiet for a moment, then added, "I'm sorry for your loss. Let me know if you need anything."

"Thank you, Sheriff. That means a lot to me, and I know Mama would be glad to know you were looking out for me."

He squeezed my shoulder and left me standing there holding the picture. I'd heard my parent's bedroom was so gruesome some officers refused to enter it. That made me want to smile but didn't, not here, not now. I would enjoy the moment when I was home alone.

"Oh, before I go," the sheriff said, walking back toward me. "Can I have a DNA sample so that we can rule you out?" He called someone over who had items with him. "It won't hurt a bit."

"What? What do you mean?" I asked nervously.

"We found various traces of DNA, and we want to make sure it's none of the family. That way, we have a better chance of catching the guy who did this. It's just some of your saliva." He nodded, and the man opened a bag and produced something like a cotton swab to clean ears.

"Open your mouth," the man said, and I complied. He scraped the cotton swab against the inside of my cheek and placed it back inside the bag, closing it.

"What if they wore gloves?" I said, walking with the sheriff down the grassy path toward the vehicles. My stomach felt weird as I watched that man hurry off with my DNA sample.

"Well, that's what we want to find out," he said, opening his car door. "The labs are still small and there are backlogs, therefore testing may not even be done, but I wanted to get everything ready so that when they were available, we didn't waste any time. I want to close this case as soon as possible. For closure, for you."

"Thank you, Sheriff. I appreciate you taking on this case personally." I waved him goodbye and headed for my car.

I never heard from the sheriff and after his death—which I helped along, thanks to my potent oil—nobody else took over and it became another cold case.

And I would befriend someone at the police station to destroy my parent's file and all the evidence with it.

Two days later, I stood over my parent's open coffins. The moon was full, providing me with all the light I needed. There was a chill in the air, but my skin was hot and sweaty. An owl hooted above me while insects stridulated in the distance. I smelled rain along with the stench of takeout.

I wiped sweat off my brow and flinched when dirt got in my eye. I pulled out a tarp from my open trunk and unwrapped it. Then I climbed into Mama's coffin first, stared at her for a second, and in that second, I felt a smidge of the love she had given me throughout my life. But then hate washed over me and I knew I was doing the right thing.

Bending my knees, I picked Mama up and gagged. Her smell was nauseating. I placed her inside the pulley system so that I didn't break my back getting her out of the hole. I did the same with Papa, placing him beside Mama so that I only had to do this once.

I climbed out of the hole and pulled the rope, lifting Mama and Papa out of their graves. Once they were wrapped tightly in their own tarp, I lifted their bodies into my trunk, closed their graves, and packed up my equipment.

I neatened Mama's blue floral dress, ensuring it covered her knees, then covered them both with their duvet.

I stood at the foot of their bed, watching them sleep peacefully.

It was the first time in a really long time that I was happy entering their room. There was no shouting, no cruel words spewed at me, and no hurtful glances. It was calm.

And the itch at the back of my neck had stopped.

But only for a while…

Next in the Steve Campbell Psychological Suspense Thriller Series

vinci-books.com/boneforest

In the heart of the forest, the dead don't stay buried—and the truth is even darker.

When the body of a woman from Boise is discovered brutally murdered in the Sawtooth Forest, Detective Steve Campbell fears the work of a cult.

Turn the page for a free preview…

The Bone Forest: Chapter One

DON'T TRUST THE DEVIL EVEN THOUGH YOU KNOW HIM

The Dominant

Melissa closed her eyes as she succumbed to the pleasures her dominant was inflicting on her.

"What's your color?" he asked in a deep tone.

"Green," she said breathlessly.

"Do you want me to do it again?" he asked, this time with his lips close to her ear so he could watch all the hairs on the back of her neck and shoulders stand on end.

"Yes, please, Sir," she whimpered, licking dry lips.

The dominant leaned forward, kissed her left shoulder, then walked around her where he checked the leather restraints securing her wrists and ankles to the St. Andrew's cross; they were tight but not enough to stop blood flow.

Grabbing the crop from the hook on the wall, the dominant slapped it into his hand, creating a sharp snap sound, making his submissive flinch. His hand stung, but it wasn't hard; it had more sound than bite, so he knew it wouldn't cause harm.

He returned to Melissa and administered soft taps across her shoulder blades and then buttocks, each getting successively harder until leaving red welts across her soft, pink flesh. With each slap of the crop against her skin, Melissa cried out in pleasurable moans, which pleased the dominant. What pleased him even more was watching her porcelain skin turn rosy, each welt raising slightly with soft hairs standing up.

The dominant hung the crop back and reached for the flogger. "Color?" he asked again, ensuring his submissive was pleasantly happy with his delicious torture.

Melissa was quiet for a while as she collected her thoughts. "Green, Sir," she finally said, licking her lips. She swallowed hard and licked her lips again. He couldn't see her eyes behind the black satin blindfold, but her parted lips, rosy cheeks, and the sweat peppering her forehead told him exactly where she was.

The dominant loved it when a submissive reacted this way; when they were well on their way into the depths of their inner, yet soft, darkness. To a place where they felt safe, secure, and utterly comfortable. A place where they forgot about the world, a place where they thought about nothing but the pleasures he inflicted on her body. This place was their subspace; and he held the key to unlocking the ecstasy of her deep submission.

Melissa moaned with each whip of the dominant's soft leather flogger. It didn't hurt, but with a flick of his wrist, the ends of the leather tails whipped flesh, creating a sharp, short bite. He continued his pleasurable assault on her back, creating a rhythmic dance of leather against her skin, sending her further into the dark depths of her inner soul.

He returned the flogger on the wall, her back and buttocks a deep red, and closed the gap between them, pausing to let the anticipation build. In a single fluid move a ponytail twisted around one hand, snapping her head to one side. He thrust his tongue down her throat, owning her; and his little submissive absorbed him, moaning softly in his kiss, intensifying when his free hand reached down between her legs held wide by spreader bars.

A finger continued teasing her, playing with that little button between her legs, but before sending her over the edge, he tightened the belt around her neck, ensuring the chain and locket were out of the way. Melissa's mouth opened as she fought to take in air. He licked her top lip, and pressed the Hitachi Magic Wand against her swollen clit until sparks flew and she cried out when her orgasm smashed into her over and over again.

The belt around her neck tightened even more, cutting off her air completely. The satin blindfold was lifted so she could see him. Melissa stared at him with pleading eyes, unable to loosen the restraints herself. She convulsed and shook but nothing helped, and the more the belt tightened, the more she thrashed around until finally her oxygen-starved body stilled, her eyes unseeing.

The Bone Forest: Chapter Two

A HIKER'S SURPRISE

Donovan caught up to his barking dog and rubbed his head. "Who's a good boy?" Donovan said, rubbing his dog behind his ears. "Yes, you're a good boy. Now what are you barking at?"

Donovan glanced up at the crown shyness of the trees and smiled, even in nature trees avoided each other much like himself avoiding his problems, and other people. Instead, he preferred hiking with Bob by his side.

The air smelled of pines, wet leaves, and rain, even though there wasn't a cloud in the sky. He inhaled deeply, exhaled, and shivered. His frown deepened as he raised his head and sniffed again. There was the smell again, which he couldn't place.

"Is that what you're smelling, Bob?" Donovan said, connecting the leash to his dog's collar. As much as he loved watching Bob run around on his own, that smell left him worried and wanted to ensure Bob's safety as much as his own. He sniffed again and cringed. "That's a nasty stench, boy."

Bob barked again and pulled Donovan off the Sawtooth Forest hiking trail near Bald Mountain. Donovan yanked on the leash to slow Bob down, but the dog was adamant that they reached the offending area immediately.

Donovan followed Bob, who sniffed under logs, around bushes, and near trees, until finally they reached an area where the stench was greatest. The ground at their feet had dried leaves strewn everywhere, but what laid on top made Donovan gag and turn around.

Bob continued sniffing and pawing at the animal carcass. From the looks of it, another predator had ripped the animal apart and left it there for later; or that's what Donovan thought and a reason he wanted to leave.

"Come now," Donovan said, yanking on the leash. "Leave it alone."

Bob continued pawing at the carcass on top of the mound of leaves, moving dirt around, and revealing something that made Donovan's blood drain from every part of his body. He couldn't tear his eyes away from the fingers sticking out of the ground or the worn, dark maroon polish on her nails.

Donovan swallowed the lump in his throat and pulled the leash hard enough to make Bob yelp and sit near his owner. Crouching, Donovan picked up a stick and poked at the hand and quickly realized it was human and not a mannequin he had hoped it was. He jumped backward, tripping over a rock, and fell hard on his bum. Donovan bolted upright and glanced around, ensuring he was the only one here, and pulled out his cell phone.

The Bone Forest: Chapter Three

THE BODY DUMP

Detective Steve Campbell

I placed my dishes in the sink and turned in time to catch Alice by her waist before she exited the kitchen and pulled her in for an embrace.

"It's a pity you need to leave," she said with her arms around my neck, glancing up at me. She gave me a look that tore at my heartstrings, and I'd do anything to stay at home with her for a day and garden or go for a walk or even just sitting around talking. Her light-brown eyes held sadness, and I wanted to kiss the hurt away.

I leaned forward and kissed her on the tip of her nose. "I'll be home for dinner," I said, smiling. With everything she had gone through, I enjoyed keeping things light at home and not so serious. "What are your plans for today?" I asked in a cheerful tone.

"Not sure, but I might go to the market today," she said, resting her head against my chest and squeezed me.

We had moved to Ketchum eight months ago, and with

each passing week, she started leaving the house more frequently. Last year, Alice had suffered two miscarriages, and the doctor advised us not to try again for a few months. Ever since then, she hadn't been well, and had been deteriorating by falling into a deep depression.

Then, the last case I had worked on, the man responsible for kidnapping all those women, had sent Alice a sunflower, a way to threaten me into leaving him alone. To protect Alice, I asked a doctor to admit Alice into high care at the local hospital to keep her safe but also to treat her. It was short of a miracle what he had done for her because a few days later she came home a little healthier and happier.

Although she wasn't herself one hundred percent, she was healing one day at a time, and when she had good days like today and ventured out, it warmed my heart. That meant that one day soon I'd have my Alice back. The woman I fell in love with in school, and love still. What we had was something different, in my mind. It was a love that connected us on a soul level, and not just skin deep.

"Have a good day at the market," I said, kissing her forehead.

"Do you know what kind of scene it is?" she asked, looking up at me with concern etched on her face.

"They found something near Bald Mountain in Sawtooth Forest they want me to look at."

"I hope it's not bad," she said solemnly, glancing away.

Not wanting to make her day worse, I smiled, cupped her face, and kissed her gently. "I'll see when I get there." She knew I solved homicide cases for a living; therefore I said nothing else about any new case I worked on. From experience, anything found in or near a forest usually meant it was a murder scene. Alice had been through enough. The last thing she needed now was to hear about a woman brutally tortured and murdered.

I parked my car behind Officer Graham's vehicle; it was the only one with a pink bunny on the back window; it was something his 4-year-old toddler had demanded he left in his personal car for protection.

I smiled at the thought of having a toddler running around giving me teddies to keep me safe, then sadness washed over me because we may never have a child of our own. We could always adopt, but I would first see how Alice recovered before bringing up the subject. Any topic that revolved around children made her teary and, although I wasn't in a rush to have a child, we were both in our forties, which made things difficult for us.

I walked past his vehicle to get to the hiking trail and remembered why I was here. Although I'd been to many crime scenes, this time it felt different; Alice still needed me at home, but I needed to work. This would be my third case in Ketchum, and a hiker and his dog found the body off the hiking trail, and the way Officer Graham had explained the crime scene it left me on edge.

"Detective," James McIntosh said, our lab technician who always got to scenes before me. "How's Alice doing?"

"Better every day," I said, shaking his gloved hand. "How was your vacation?"

"Those four days in Hawaii were so wonderful that I've already booked our next trip there," he said, grinning. "If hubby had found a job while we were there, he would've taken it on the spot and we'd move without thinking twice."

He took the disposable gloves off and threw them in a trash bag he was carrying.

"It would be our loss," I said, walking on the hiking path beside him. "Aren't you happy here?"

"It's not me, Detective," James said, staring at his boots as we walked. "Hubby needs to get out of the situation he's in. His boss is toxic, the environment is toxic. Everything about that place is awful."

"I hope he finds something closer, though. Not sure what we would do without you," I said sincerely. James was a wonderful crime scene technician, and it would be a significant loss to the team if he chose to leave.

James smiled. "Thanks," he glanced in my direction, "I appreciate that."

"What do we have?" I said, changing the subject and jerking my chin in the direction we were heading.

He shook his head and handed me a fresh pair of disposable gloves. "He covered her in a shallow grave with the carcass of a fox on top of her body."

"I wonder if he did that to hide her scent?"

"Probably," James said, walking off the path. "She has ligature marks all over her body."

I frowned. "Do you think they used rope?"

"I'm not sure. Probably. But I think the new coroner is best to answer your questions."

I'd forgotten about the new coroner starting today. "Dr. R. Brink," I said, more to myself than to James.

"Yep, we said our goodbyes to Doc Lesley early this morning when he came in to fetch his belongings and introduced us to the new Doc. She seems nice."

I stared at James as we walked, thinking the R was for Richard, but apparently the R in Dr. R. Brink was for someone female. I smiled to myself. We had more than enough men in the department. Having a female coroner would be a breath of fresh air.

"Over here," James said, pointing at his equipment on the ground, the bright lights on the scene, and where her body was.

"Morning," Officer Graham said, tipping his head, placing a marker on the ground, then placing the wrapper inside an evidence bag for processing.

"Morning," I said. "Is it just us today?"

"Yeah, Officer Crick is searching the area, and the other lab technicians are busy with another scene, so I'm helping James collect evidence."

I stood a distance away from the crime scene and glanced around. The killer had placed the victim near a large tree far from the hiking trail but still close to the parking area, and covered her with dirt and leaves. The roots of the tree seemed to shield her body from the elements, almost hugging her in nature's coffin. It was a strange scene to witness. Something I'd never seen before.

James continued collecting evidence while Officer Graham placed markers around the scene. Officer Graham took pictures and collected evidence that might reveal something, but I doubted it. Some of the wrappers collected could've been left there by other hikers.

I stepped closer to the victim to see what we were dealing with and I did everything I could not to turn away. Sand and leaves dirtied her knotty blond hair. Her blue-colored eyes were no longer vibrant but dull and unseeing. There were bruises along both sides of her jaw, on the left-hand side of her cheek, and a cut above her left eyebrow. Then, glancing lower, there was bruising around her neck, wrists, and ankles. The killer had sliced her right breast, splitting it in two. It seemed barbaric and done in anger.

She was slightly on the large side yet seemed healthy, apart from being murdered.

"Do you think the killer had strangled her to death?" I asked James, who was collecting evidence off her body.

"I honestly don't know," he said, shaking his head. "The killer had sexually assaulted her and there are wounds on her back."

I sucked in a deep breath of forest air and walked around the markers Officer Graham had placed on the ground. Glancing up, I noticed the trees above us kept their distance from the next tree. The air was cool, with a fine mist rolling in from the north. The hiking path was a few meters away which, when traversing it, one could enjoy breathtaking views of Ketchum, but there was nothing enjoyable about this view.

"Do we have a name for her?" I asked, standing near James.

"Melissa King, twenty-nine years old," James said, raising the evidence bag holding her identity, then he placed it in the box with the rest of the items he had collected. "At least the killer was decent enough to leave her handbag with all her things inside. It makes our job slightly easier." I detected a hint of sarcasm and I didn't blame him. The sooner we identified victims the sooner we could notify relatives.

The longer I stared at the victim, the angrier I became. "Christ, who did she provoke to suffer such a savage killing?" I asked, swallowing my breakfast that threatened to repeat on me.

James stood and dusted leaves and soil off his gloves. "My sister's kid is her age," he said sadly. "They even have similar hair color." He pointed at our victim's hair, then quickly glanced away.

The Last Girl

In our line of work we shouldn't find resemblance in a victim to a family member. Usually it made our work that much harder. But it was difficult to not be human and to see the victim as a person we might have known. I needed to focus on something else and started making notes in my book.

"I think I got them all," Officer graham said, placing evidence bags in the box for James.

"Thanks," James said, crouching again. "I should be done soon and then I'll remove her body when the coroner arrives."

"Detective!" Officer Crick yelled.

I spun around as he jogged toward us. "What did you find?" I asked, closing the gap.

"I found a shrine of sorts," he pointed to my right, "and I think I found a pool of blood." He stopped walking to catch his breath and thumbed behind him.

"Well, come on. Show me," I said, jogging past him.

Officer Crick groaned, turned around, and caught up to me.

"Officer Graham!" I yelled, calling him over. "We'll need help to collect evidence for James."

"Take this," James called out to Officer Graham, who waited for the items. "And take pictures before you collect."

"Will do," Officer Graham said, running after us.

Grab your copy...
vinci-books.com/boneforest

About the Author

Multi-genre author writing twisted endings...

N Gray is a USA Today Bestselling Author who lives in Cape Town, South Africa, with her daughter and adopted cat named Miss Beans.

During the day, she's an analyst and provider profiler for a medical insurance company. At night, she types on her curved keyboard, creating fictional characters some may love and others you want to kill yourself.

She writes in four genres: urban fantasy, thriller, horror, and paranormal romance.

She now writes under Natalie Michaels for her new thrillers and SD Syns for her new horrors.

Acknowledgments

Thank you to my readers, old and new, for taking a chance on my books.

You are the reason I write the stories I do. As long as you keep reading, I'll keep writing.

I'm truly humbled by your support and encouragement.